W9-CBV-706

Deep Purple

By Mayra Montero

DEEP PURPLE

THE RED OF HIS SHADOW

THE LAST NIGHT I SPENT WITH YOU

IN THE PALM OF DARKNESS

THE MESSENGER

Deep Purple

a novel

Mayra Montero

TRANSLATED FROM THE SPANISH

BY EDITH GROSSMAN

An Imprint of HarperCollins*Publishers*

DEEP PURPLE. Copyright © 2003 by Mayra Montero. English translation © by Edith Grossman. All rights reserved. Printed in the United States of America. No part of this book may be used or reproduced in any manner whatsoever without written permission except in the case of brief quotations embodied in critical articles and reviews. For information address Harper-Collins Publishers Inc., 10 East 53rd Street, New York, NY 10022.

HarperCollins books may be purchased for educational, business, or sales promotional use. For information, please write: Special Markets Department, HarperCollins Publishers Inc., 10 East 53rd Street, New York, NY 10022.

FIRST EDITION

Originally published in Spanish by Tusquets as
Púrpura profundo.

Designed by Cassandra J. Pappas

Printed on acid-free paper

Library of Congress Cataloging-in-Publication Data
Montero, Mayra, 1952–
   [Púrpura profundo. English]
   Deep purple : a novel / Mayra Montero ; translated from the Spanish by Edith Grossman.
     p. cm.
   ISBN 0-06-093821-8
    I. Grossman, Edith, 1936–   II. Title.
PQ7440.M56 P8713 2003
863'.64—dc21   2002040837

03 04 05 06 07 BVG/QBM 10 9 8 7 6 5 4 3 2
1

For Jorge

"Nocturnes" are melancholy!
"Marches" are harsh!
"Overtures" soon
are "apertures"!

—LUIS DE TAPAI,
 "Music"

Nothing endures
but the pleasure and texture
of an instant: that is my motto.

—SEVERO SARDUY,
 "A Transient Witness in Disguise"

Deep Purple

Saying good-bye to one's profession is like saying good-bye to sex, one clings to it, I cling to this brief piece of writing as if it were a woman's body, the last I will ever embrace in my life.

I walk with a firm step through the editorial offices and notice that no one gives me a special greeting. In my heart of hearts, I expected just the opposite: that they would seem uncomfortable or nervous, afraid of seeing themselves in my mirror, and for that very reason feeling a certain urgency to be rid of me.

I don't have to ask for Sebastián, the entertainment editor. I know I'll find him in the office of the editorial writer, the most private and remote of all the offices. The man goes out for lunch between one and two o'clock, and Sebastián takes advantage of his absence to lie down under his desk, put on a mask, and take a little nap. Before he falls asleep, he leafs through the magazines that he does not dare to leaf through at home: athletes with big buttocks, extravagant mulattoes, young boys in bloom. Any day now he'll retire too, and when he leaves his profession he'll leave his magazines as well: the torsos he lightly caresses with his fingertips, the thighs he will never bite, the bellies that will never experience the licking of his aged tongue. When he leaves the paper, he'll leave everything he desired in silence. I am leaving; I desired in silence, but I have also attained my desires: quietly I have devoured the world. Or so I've wanted to believe.

"Sebastián," I call. "Are you awake?"

In addition to the mask, he has a plush band tied around his forehead. The band is soaked in bay rum, and that means a migraine has dug its claws into him.

"Here's my last piece," I say, and I lay the papers on the desk.

"The photographs arrived," he replies, removing his mask.

The band soaked in bay rum is the only vice he owes to

his wife. That, at least, is what Gloria, his wife, says; a teacher of English literature, she is a phlegmatic, subtle woman who knows very well what she has at home. All women try not to know, but deep down they do.

"You should have kept count," Sebastián says to me, half-opening his eyes. "With all the virtuosas you fucked, you could have formed your own band."

"One or two male soloists fell too," I admit, relishing his surprise ahead of time. Or perhaps he isn't surprised?

Sebastián laughs, but as if he were slightly shocked. I know I've plucked a dangerous string, and he sits up in order to hear better. Then I think I ought to give him this happiness. For him, too, it must be happiness.

"It was about twenty years ago. He was an Australian pianist—perhaps you remember him—he wore his hair in a little knot in back."

He stands and shakes out his trousers, very carefully, to gain time. I look only at his expectant face, those eyes that have filled up with an intense, melancholy astonishment.

"Of course, he loosened the knot. His back was white, very white, and his hands were freckled."

"I remember that pianist," Sebastián murmurs, and he

begins to chew for no reason, a gesture that means nothing but old age.

"Clint Verret." I say his name curtly. "And I assure you he wasn't the only one."

He shakes his head, trying to appear incredulous. But at this point, with my final review lying on the desk, which is like saying with the barrel of a revolver pressing against my temple, he knows I'm incapable of lying.

"I followed him to Denver. We spent three days there."

"You must be ready to die," Sebastián prognosticates. "I can't believe you're making a confession."

"I'm already dead," I say to him quietly. "When I finished writing that review I died of despair."

We both know what I will have to endure now. In less than five minutes they'll call me to the managing editor's office, I'll go there as if I didn't suspect a thing, and I'll find a little farewell party. Some people will try to console me: they'll talk about how lucky I am to be able to travel, and how much I'll enjoy my grandchildren, and what a delight it will be to sit down and read the books I didn't have time to read before. I won't tell them that I don't travel anymore; my wife insists, but I've lost interest. Or that I have no desire to devote myself to my daughter's children, taking them to shopping centers and buying them trinkets; who wants to grow old like an idiot? Or that at this stage of my life I have no reason to start reading the books I once ignored. I want to do exactly what I was doing when they suggested I retire: teach orchestral history and literature at the conservatory, and write music criticism for the paper. My work at the conservatory ended some months ago, but I had hoped to continue writing my reviews. I possess all the necessary experience, and I'll bet that after so many years I'm the only one who has the perfect dose of malice. I know how to gauge musicians from the first moment I see them. With a woman, I look at how she raises her shoulders, or the manner in which she purses her mouth. With a man, I always notice his crotch, and in particular how he moves his thumbs.

"Write your memoirs or something," Sebastián suggests. "Didn't you say you were keeping notes for a book? Write it, Agustín, do it now. We can sign it with a pseudonym."

Sebastián includes himself so that I'll feel that he's my accomplice. I've already had the same thought: to write a kind of notebook, or diary, and tell the story of Virginia

Tuten, the true story of what she and I lived through together; the engulfing vortex of Manuela Suggia, all the horror of her end; my relations with Clint Verret, that amorous, depraved man; the dangerous manias of Rebecca Cheng, by far the best clarinetist who ever passed through this city. And my arms.

Mati, the managing editor's secretary, interrupts us: her boss is waiting and I ought to hurry. I say yes, with sad eyes, as if I had just been advised that my funeral is about to take place. Sebastián gives a mocking little laugh, and I look at him for the last time; for the last time as the good critic I've been. I need to know I was the best. Or not; I don't need anybody to tell me. I know I was good, or perhaps special, and that happened because most of the time I judged musicians for their instincts; I evaluated their gifts as performers in a different way: besides listening to their music, I smelled them, I heard them speak, I listened to the rumble of their intestines. It may sound prosaic, but one's musical soul lies in the guts: I could confirm this on the spot by placing my ear there and listening carefully.

Sebastián has an old, gray mustache that looks fake, and a thick head of hair that's also gray. His eyes are rather sunken—at our age everything sinks—and his cheeks are flaccid. He looks like an Indian with the plush band tied around his head.

"All you need is the feather," I say before I'm dragged away by fat Romero, the sports editor.

As soon as they see me my colleagues applaud and shake my hand, and some pat me on the shoulder. Ibsen, the society editor, hands me a box wrapped in gift paper. I open the box and move tissue paper aside until I find the pajama top. It is made of blue satin and has my initials embroidered on it. The pajamas remind me of others, the ones Virginia Tuten was wearing on the afternoon she opened the door to me. She also wore a pearl necklace, but that is part of the story I'm going to tell about the beauty I've kept to myself for so many years, or the horrors I'll vomit up until my soul crumples.

Mejías, the editor in chief, gives me my next-to-last review in a silver frame, with an engraved inscription. I avoid reading it; I suspect it's a depressing little paragraph. The new music critic, a young kid, looks at me with something resembling gratitude, but it could also be relief; and the managing editor, in order to say something, says please not to forget them.

"I'll come by to write every once in a while," I reply in a

thin little voice, but no one pays attention. If they did, there would be no reason to have a farewell party; my announced retirement would be a kind of joke, and the world would have no order, or destiny, or fatality.

Finally, someone insists that I say a few words. I feel ridiculous, almost immoral, holding the blue pajamas in my hands.

"I'll probably write a book," I say, "but not my memoirs. A few remarks about the musicians I knew . . ."

There is more applause; canapés are passed around and some plastic glasses filled with red wine. As the celebration comes to an end (what are we celebrating?) I feel as if my gravestone is being lowered. I need air, but I'll be back very soon. I'll come back for my notes, my papers, even a wisp of hair (pubic hair, the only kind that matters) that belonged to Alejandrina Sanromá, the genius of the celeste.

Sebastián takes my arm and offers to walk with me to my car. We go out into the corridor, we take the elevator without saying a word. Suddenly I burst into laughter.

"She used to suckle a bat," I gasp; my laughter barely permits me to speak.

"Who?" asks Sebastián.

"That woman who played the French horn, Clarissa Berdsley; have you ever put your mouth where that animal placed his?"

Sebastián throws his head back just as the elevator doors open.

"Not often, dear boy. To my sorrow, not often."

Virginia

A CHINESE VIOLINIST WHO was passing through San Juan opened his shirt and showed me what from that moment on I called the "mark of Saint-Saëns." It was a thick, dark red line that ran along the base of his neck, on the left, above the collarbone, and could have been mistaken for something else—the mark left by a stained finger, for example, or an old burn.

He assured me that his was not one of the most serious. Other violinists also had irritated skin there, in the place where they rested the violin, and with the friction—or the passion of certain melodies—blisters formed, lacerations of varying degrees of severity that occasionally became infected. He added that he had heard of a Russian virtuoso for whom the interpretation of certain pieces by Saint-Saëns caused such intense discomfort that sometimes, when the concert was over, the doctors were obliged to administer morphine.

I underlined this fact and saved it for my files. After spending so much time pestering musicians who may or may not have known what they were saying, I chose to keep the best secrets for myself and take the rest to the paper, the minimum that people expect, not too many, and never anything personal. I have an outstanding collection of indiscretions and unusual remarks. Their fans would be amazed if they knew the carnal—or should I say carnivorous?—terms in which some soloists express themselves with regard to their instruments, or the music they interpret.

On that occasion, the Chinese violinist was surprised when I bent over to look at the mark on his neck. There are only two images that astound us for the rest of our lives. One has to do with death: generally it is the mouth, the eyelids, or the hands of a dead family member. The other has to do with desire, or, I should say, with the presentiment of desire.

Seeing it up close, on skin that for a moment was neither yellow nor white, neither a man's nor a woman's, I
longed to smell and kiss the mark of the violin, the dam-
age it had done. I closed my eyes, in a kind of trance, and
felt that something distant and not completely mine was
toying with me. The violinist interpreted my gesture in
another fashion and moved away, perplexed. But it was
not until I met Virginia, several years later, that I discovered that this incident had its justified hazard. I was taught
the concept of justified hazard some time ago by a Brazil-
ian guitarist, and at first it seemed a nonsensical idea, but
gradually I began to grasp its meaning. And I came to
understand it completely on the morning I saw Virginia
for the first time.

I arrived at the theater when the rehearsal had already
begun. I made my way between the empty seats and sat at
the end of the ninth row, which I have been in the habit
of doing ever since I began this job. I believe in always
attending rehearsals, even when I'm perfectly familiar
with the soloist. But in the case of Virginia, the truth was
that I didn't know her at all; I had not heard any of her
recordings, or even looked at the photograph that had
been sent to the paper along with her biography.

For that reason, because I had assumed she was American and did not even suspect that she had been born in Antigua—Virginia Tuten is the only soloist I know of from that unexpected tropical hideaway—I was surprised when I saw a corpulent mulatta, an opulent wet nurse who was playing, in my opinion without much spirit, *Salut d'amour*, Elgar's most cloying piece.

I half-closed my eyes and then I thought of the "mark of Saint-Saëns." In a flash I pictured it as somewhat shorter, perhaps thicker, much paler, on the skin of this woman. She finished playing and moved her head from side to side, the movement of an impatient colt that violinists use to relax their neck muscles. Then she went over to the pianist and together they began to look at some detail of the score. She stood sideways, and instead of looking at her breasts, which were of a remarkable structure and density, I lowered my eyes and remarked on her feet.

Feet tell me a good deal about the musical character of a violinist. I notice the size and shape, and the manner in which the musician brings them together or separates them; I also look carefully at the calves, and somehow I know that the musician's expressiveness comes from there,

from the ankles and the backs of the knees. On the afternoon of the rehearsal, Virginia was wearing white espa-
drilles: I cannot conceive of anything sweeter or more
appropriate for a violinist about to submerge herself, like a
nymph, in *La Fontaine d'Aréthuse*. That was the moment
when I felt an urgent need to leave the ninth row and sit
closer to the stage, and in the middle of the row: for the
first time in my career, I had, and gave in to, the temptation to make myself noticeable.

Before she began to rehearse the second part, I heard
her tell the pianist that she would take a break. I didn't
move from my seat until I saw her disappear, dragging her
feet slightly, and I realized that either she was not very
agile or was one of the musicians who lowered her tone in
rehearsal. Some sopranos and tenors rehearse in whispers
in order not to strain their voices; sometimes violinists
control their sudden movements, remain silent in order to
concentrate, take light meals, and refrain from sex the
night before a performance.

I asked myself, as I knocked at the door of her dressing
room, if Virginia Tuten also had so many idiosyncrasies. I
went on asking myself the question when the door was

opened by a robust blond woman, evidently an American, and I had the suspicion—more than a suspicion, a sly, cruel certainty—that I had just interrupted something important. You can smell it; anyone who decides to can smell it. I saw her damp neck and wrinkled skirt, and in case that wasn't enough, I saw those crafty eyes, that thirst so typical of a male. I smiled to myself: the blonde who introduced herself as the violinist's secretary in reality had been kissing her, caressing the breasts of the great virtuosa, begging her to calm down. Perhaps Virginia Tuten was too tense. As they grow older, female violinists, I don't know why, become insecure. It should be the reverse—with pianists it's the reverse—but with violinists the opposite happens: the younger they are, the bolder. And then they become timid; they dim a little each day until they retire, generally at an age younger than the men.

"Virginia isn't feeling well," said the blonde, after I identified myself and reminded her that we had an appointment. "She's rather tense. Couldn't you interview her this afternoon?"

I smiled, trying to look like an idiot. I realized that in

order to get to the violinist, I had to get past the barrier of a she-lion burning with desire. I am—or was—an intuitive music critic. I said it would be no problem for me to wait until the afternoon, and perhaps it would be even better because then the photographer could take Virginia's picture on the hotel grounds, surrounded by peacocks, or strolling along the beach.

The woman swallowed the bait. In those days I was strong; I had black hair, impeccable manners, and a fashionably large mustache. I wasn't a weakling; I mean, I didn't look like a fanatic music lover, much less a music critic. Someone more sophisticated would have sensed the claws behind my cordiality. But my way of speaking, my willingness to be obliging and hold the interview somewhere other than the theater, as was the custom, undoubtedly led her to believe that she was in the presence of a harmless man. She closed the door and my expression must have changed. I imagined her returning to the side of the violinist and telling her that she had managed to get rid of a reporter, a pest who had insisted on seeing her at the hotel at about five. Virginia, her eyes closed, would remain silent. Then her secretary would take advantage of the opportunity to kiss her on the lips—a gentle but very dangerous kiss—and allow her to rest for a few minutes before resuming the rehearsal.

I called the paper, requested a photographer, and went to my class at the conservatory. Shortly after noon I went home: my wife had not returned yet from her office, and the girl was practicing the piano under the supervision of my mother-in-law. I took a bath and changed my clothes, and before I went out again I looked up some facts about Edward Elgar. *Salut d'amour* had been composed for his student Alice, and they would play it together: Elgar on the violin and Alice at the piano. It was all the information of what we might call an intimate nature that I had. But in a sense it was enough, and I thought that with it I could cook up something marvelous.

I kissed my daughter and had that shuddering presentiment I always had when I saw her at the piano: suppose one day she became a successful concert pianist and fell into the hands of an old fox like me? Suppose that fox told her an apocryphal story about the love affair of Béla Bartók with a young girl whom he undressed and smeared with a mixture of chocolate and palinka, the Hungarian liqueur the color of blood, so that he could lick her and chew her to pieces?

I bent over the girl, corrected the posture of her back, and recommended that she pay attention to the position of her left hand. I asked my mother-in-law not to let her out of her sight. They both smiled and I felt miserable. I left the house and looked for a cab. In those days I almost always traveled by taxi. I had learned to drive as a boy, but for certain plans a car could sometimes be an obstacle. A soloist would never get into a car driven by a music critic she didn't know; it's a tacit rule that is rarely broken, and then only by cellists. Don't ask me why they are the ones and not, for example, women who play the clarinet or those dedicated to the oboe. Cellists have a more open attitude toward almost everything. And the idea of getting into a car with a critic who may crucify them the next day, musically speaking, does not seem to bother them.

At a quarter to five I arrived at the Caribe Hilton, crossed the lobby, and went to the house phone to call Virginia Tuten's room. I counted six rings, but there was no answer. I checked the room number with one of the desk clerks; I called again—eight rings this time—and no one picked up the phone. It was impossible that they hadn't come back yet from rehearsal. Female violinists generally don't go shopping; they don't stop off at some restaurant; it doesn't even occur to them to take a walk in the city. They are all in a hurry to return to the hotel, continue rehearsing alone, and order a light meal; with it they usually drink mineral water. I have known a good number of them, I have seen them move around the room; I myself have gotten up to accept the tray with her food and allow the naked virtuosa, still holding her bow, to hide in the bathroom until the waiter leaves.

I decided to go up to the room, on the eighth floor. My mouth was dry and I wanted to stop at the bar and have a beer, but I had the feeling that time was not in my favor, a feeling that wasn't normal, because the interview would be done today or it probably would never be done, and in the long run it didn't matter very much. I knocked at the door and no one answered for quite some time. I stayed there, rubbing my knuckles, sensing that sooner or later the door was going to open. Then I heard a moan: "Who is it?" I knocked again, and the moaning sounded more distant, as if the person making the sound was moving away from the door instead of coming closer to it. There was another silence that lasted two or three minutes, and at the end of that time I realized someone was trying to open the door. A clumsy, torpid attempt. I thought I would see Virginia's secretary again, the avaricious she-lion who by now had surely been satisfied: she had even had time to take a nap with the violinist. I can attest to the fact that there is no deeper pleasure, no more extravagant and refined lasciviousness, than that derived from awaking, in the middle of the afternoon, at the side of a virtuosa. In the darkened room, when we sit up in bed and observe that body at rest, that flesh that a few hours earlier had vibrated as it played the cello, the piano, the perverse harpsichord, we are assailed by a feeling of impotence, but, at the same time, we are shaken by the possibility of a frenzied ecstasy, of a temblor rarely savored. That is when we feel the urgent need to waken the virtuosa (or virtuoso, a small, dozing male musician) and massacre, bury, drown her in imprecations and threats. As for me, I must admit that on occasion I have wanted to give free rein to my cruelty; I have longed to open that body and bury my face in the warm opening—temperament is in the entrails—and win the match against a passion that is no longer hers, or mine, or anyone's. Tearing out the musical soul is all that is desired.

A prudent Virginia Tuten, with dark circles under her eyes, opened the door slightly without removing the little security chain. She was in pajamas, blue satin pajamas. In a tearful voice she asked what I wanted.

"I'm Agustín Cabán," I said. "I came to interview you this morning. Your secretary suggested an appointment this afternoon."

She asked me to wait a moment. She closed the door and I looked at my watch. The photographer was coming at five-thirty, but it was obvious that the violinist was in no condition for photographs. I leaned against the wall and wanted to smoke: it was the relief of knowing that the secretary would not be there. I waited five, ten minutes. Virginia returned and opened the door. She had taken off her pajamas and put on a long-sleeved yellow robe that fastened up to the neck. I had the impression, in the faint light from the balcony, that her face was red. Next to her left ear, almost at the level of her jaw, I thought I could make out a bruise. I looked away and we both stood there, she not knowing what to say and I not knowing if I could sit down.

"Where would you like to do the interview?" I asked. I looked around; everything was in disorder.

She did not answer right away. She picked up the clothes that were on a chair, went to the far end of the room, and came back carrying her violin case.

"If you like," I added, "we can do it on the beach."

She was deciding something, staring down at the floor. Suddenly she looked up.

"Get me out of here before they kill me."

I opened my mouth; I don't know how long I stood there with my mouth open, trying to digest that statement. All I remember is that when I came to, I closed it with a snap. Once again I felt confident, strong, and determined to save her.

"Get dressed and we'll leave."

Before my eyes, Virginia Tuten took off her robe. She was wearing the most ordinary white underwear, the kind an older woman would wear, though I estimated she was no more than thirty or thirty-five years old. She turned her back to me and I remember thinking that it would have been a waste if anyone had killed her. I made an effort to remain still as she rummaged through her things and haphazardly pulled out articles of clothing. In a minute she was dressed in a skirt and blouse, and then I saw her put on a jacket and a pair of high-heeled black shoes. She even had the presence of mind to put on a pearl necklace. I thought that only a very unhappy and very fragile woman would be capable of remembering a pearl necklace under circumstances like these.

"Let's go," she said, holding her purse in one hand and her violin case in the other.

I opened the door, we went out to the corridor, and as soon as we were in the elevator I whispered my plan:

"We'll do the interview at another hotel, what do you think?"

She nodded yes and said in a little girl's voice:

"Anywhere else I know I'll be safe."

"TELL ME ABOUT Clint Verret." Sebastián leaned over my shoulder to look at the computer screen. There was my piece, the continuation of my mad history with Virginia Tuten. "Or didn't anything happen with Verret?"

"I told you that he loosened his knot," I replied. "And that he had enormous freckled hands. You weren't aware of how big they were until you saw him play."

A week after my forced retirement, I went back to the paper. People weren't even surprised. In Editorial it's always this way. After the little farewell parties, those who have retired disappear for a week or two. Then they come back with the excuse that they're picking up their mail. And then, inevitably, they stop for a few minutes at their desk (what had been their desk for many years), they sit down to look over papers, they turn on the computer to see if they've left any stories unfinished. The next thing is a visit to the morgue to consult old newspapers; they all pretend they're doing research to write a book. Since that takes some time, before they know it it's time for lunch and they go down to the cafeteria. Once they are there, their life returns to normal: the same table, the same colleagues, the comments on politics and sports. Nobody seems too surprised by their return; nobody asks them if they still plan to travel or devote more time to their grandchildren.

I myself concluded that it wasn't worth concealing anything, and I went directly to see Sebastián. I told him I couldn't write at home (at least, not the memoirs I was interested in writing) and that I had to do it at the paper. All I needed was a computer and a quiet corner where I could work in the morning, preferably from nine to twelve. At that time of day the editorial offices are half-empty. It's easy to concentrate and it's easy, above all, to remember.

"You can come whenever you like," Sebastián said grandly. "Use the desk you always used. . . . Better yet, use whichever one you want, but write something juicy. As you write you can pass the pages to me and I'll proofread them for you."

I was pleased to know he was so enthusiastic, but for the moment I needed only silence, to concentrate again on my escape with Virginia Tuten and our flight from the hotel. That day's events were whirling around my head, my own gesture when I opened the door of the cab and invited her to get in, a courtesy that allowed me to brush against her and briefly smell her hair, which was thick and curly, fastened at the back of her neck. At that moment I would have given anything to see how she would loosen it.

"I told her a story about Edward Elgar," I recalled aloud. "An incident with his student Alice."

"Knowing you," Sebastián said with a smile, "it must have been a stormy incident."

"I don't think so. I told her only that during the time he was finishing *Salut d'amour*, Elgar succumbed to a kind of fixation on noses, especially the nose of his student Alice. When they were alone for her lesson, he would lean over the little girl (she was almost a little girl), blow away the hair that fell over her forehead, lick the space between her eyebrows, and kiss her nose. He would begin by kissing it and then he would take it between his lips, cover it with his mouth, and suck on it as if it were a seed, the warm pit of a fruit that one does not wish to, or cannot, renounce. This, apparently, brought him to ecstasy; the man was consumed with passion that he spilled as tremulously as a little dove. No less a person than Alice's mother recounts this. The good woman spied on them and then made note of it in her diary."

"Verret," Sebastián recalled, "had reddish hair . . ."

"I can't go jumping from one story to the other," I replied.

"Just Verret's. Do me that little favor: write his story, and that way you'll take a break from the violinist."

I started to laugh. The Australian pianist also fastened his hair at the back of his neck; he tied it back with a rubber band. But his hair wasn't curly or thick. No, it was fine, like angel hair, but reddish-gray.

"Virginia didn't appear for her concert. I don't know if you remember the scandal."

Sebastián shook his head. Just then Malén, a little old lady who was a copy editor, came over and handed him a plastic bag filled with cut-up vegetables.

"My lunch," exclaimed Sebastián, holding up the bag. "Write whatever you want, in whatever order you like."

I looked at my watch: eleven-thirty. I stuck a note on the side of the computer: "Don't forget Virginia Tuten's background." I was referring, of course, to the violinist's relatives and to her childhood in Saint Johns, the capital of Antigua. It was necessary for me to go back that far so that the readers—or the one certain reader, who so far was Sebastián—would understand the denouement. Her father owned a small hotel, which is how he earned his living. But his true work, what he really loved, was tuning pianos. He was the only piano tuner on the island of Antigua, and he tuned barely two pianos a year, including the one in his own house. Another of his whims was that he collected miniature violins. As for her mother, she was an English pianist who, soon after her daughter's birth, ran away from her husband and Antigua, possibly following a lover. Virginia developed a liking for the violin because of her father's inoffensive miniatures, which were the only quiet, diminutive, and trustworthy objects in that house. When she was four, she asked for a real violin. She refused to sit at her mother's piano; she refused to place her hands on the keyboard. Her father took this as a gesture of loyalty. And then he ordered a custom-made violin, an instrument that would fit her tiny arms.

Virginia Tuten's arms, how beautifully they closed! How luxuriously they moved, shook, finally swooned! Her entire body swooned, but quietly, simulating a devastating coldness. She would close her eyes and I would think she had closed them forever; she was like a dead woman. I had to revive her with a little water.

I wrote another note and placed it below the first one: "Narrate details of her revival." It was almost noon, and I noticed that the editorial offices were filling up. Generally I enjoy that back-and-forth of hurrying reporters who stop by the logbook and yell at one another. But that afternoon the noise disturbed me; it interfered with my thoughts of Virginia. I gathered my things together and stood up to leave, but just then I caught sight of Sebastián sitting pathetically at his desk, picking up little pieces of vegetables and chewing them with displeasure.

"So you want the story of Clint Verret," I whispered, a little regretfully.

Sebastián couldn't hear me, but he guessed what I was whispering.

"I'm dying to read it."

Verret

WHAT THOUGHTS, what yearnings, what outlawed shadows have to be unleashed so that two men who never before desired other men suddenly recognize each other, by skin and by instinct, and throw themselves into one another's arms like creatures without memory, like savages without shame?

What could have gone through my mind when I picked up the telephone, dialed the number of a hotel in Atlanta, and asked for the room of the Australian pianist who, in a few days, would travel to San Juan to play Johannes Brahms's Second Concerto?

Nothing. All that passed through my mind were the questions I usually ask under these circumstances. We often locate the soloists in the middle of their tour, in one of the cities they visit before ours; we do a telephone interview and publish it on the day they arrive. It's not a bad tactic as far as I'm concerned. I come to rehearsal with the published interview and give it to the soloist, who usually can't read Spanish. If the soloist's a woman, and I see some possibilities in her, I offer to translate a few paragraphs. Of those who agree to listen to the translation, and the truth is there aren't many, most tend to accept my invitation to breakfast on the following day. Breakfasts, and almost nobody knows this, have more amatory possibilities than any other similar encounter, including intimate candlelit suppers. Breakfast with another person, looking into each other's eyes as you sip your coffee, ignites a subtle, astutely disguised complicity. When we've just gotten out of bed, all of us are more inclined to get back in.

Three days later Clint Verret was spreading raspberry jam on his toast and asking me, in exquisite English, how long I had been a music critic. At the time he must have been in his early thirties, and I was almost forty-eight. He had just divorced his wife, a violinist in the Sydney

Symphony Orchestra; I was celebrating my silver anniversary and helping my wife with preparations for my daughter's wedding. She was not going to be a successful concert pianist but the mother of my two grandchildren; the piano had become merely anecdotal, which, in my heart of hearts, I found reassuring. Two months earlier, Verret had lost his father. Biting into his toast, he confessed that he was still troubled by the memory of the old man dying, his staring eyes, his open mouth. I shuddered when he told me this, but I felt sorrow, a brutal solidarity, as if out of pity I wanted to embrace him, and out of compassion, suddenly, I needed to possess him.

I took another sip of coffee and then began to ask him questions: the origin of his vocation, the names of his teachers, his favorite composers. Clint Verret had a white streak in his hair, probably since the time he was a boy. But he also had more recent gray. He wore a black shirt, and his hands, so white and freckled, emerged from that fearful darkness. I invited him to take a walk along the beach; the beach is always a great excuse. At that moment I still did not dare confess to myself that Clint Verret, far from being effeminate, was a solid, masculine pianist. For that very reason, perhaps, it was so difficult to justify my longing, my tremendous desire to hold his body against mine. From the time I first saw him, first sat down beside him and breathed in his odor, I had wanted to caress Verret. I thought it was all a consequence of my age, my daughter's imminent marriage, the extreme boredom caused in me at this stage by so many women dedicated to music: at the time I had a lover in the orchestra, a married woman, the only recorder player I ever devoured in my life.

Clint Verret was the landmark, an ardent and tragic frontier. Walking beside him on the sand, I was terrified by my desire to embrace him. We talked about music and then were silent for a time. He walked ahead of me—I let him walk ahead of me—and I saw his back, the nape of his neck, which begged to be punished by me. It was like being drunk, like having had too much without intending to and suddenly vomiting up that terrible ice: only with him could I warm my belly. I told him I was going, and he asked me to stay: he wanted to show me some scores. A miserable excuse, because never in my life had I looked at scores with any soloist. I said of course, I was dying to see them, and in my heart I wanted to run into the sea; I thought the tepid water would bring me to my senses. Or was it the water, the untamable tide, that made me lose my head?

Entering a soloist's bedroom is like entering a temple. At least for me it is. Years earlier I had spent a rather long time in the suite of a famous flautist. He was already fairly old, and, of course, there was not the slightest hint of an attraction between us: we both liked women too much. But I must recognize that in the spiritual absorption, the reverence with which a music lover penetrates that intimate space, there is a very subtle ambiguity, a sexual emotion.

That was the emotion I felt when I entered Verret's room. Except that this time the emotion had nothing to do with spiritual absorption but with astounded flesh. If, instead of a famous pianist, Verret had been a gardener or a seller of combs, I would have experienced the same vertigo, an ambivalent, half-denied bliss that my soul wagered in order to sink into a labyrinth of touches and contradictions.

Verret himself proceeded with a certain reluctance, as if he had a premonition that when he walked through the door with this critic (whom he believed capable of beating him, pummeling him at the slightest innuendo), he too would have crossed a frontier in life. Verret was changing into another pianist, or another man. And I was changing into his mirror. I sat down in an armchair and he brought over the scores, which were fairly old; he showed me some notes written in the margin by Emil Gilels, a Brahms specialist. Yes, *nous aimons* Brahms, and we especially liked our indecisive closeness, the growing heat. Verret's freckled hand rested on my shoulder. I looked at it out of the corner of my eye and made this comment: "It looks like a bird." He moved his fingers—it was an involuntary movement—but he said nothing, and he did not withdraw his hand. He was behind me, and all I could hear was a very faint panting. I had an impulse to stand and knock him down. I thought I wanted to punch him— it occurred to me that I ought to—but in a matter of seconds I changed my mind: with tears in my eyes, with a yearning for something that eluded me, I turned my head and kissed his fingers.

Pianists, out of instinct, shelter their hands; in bed, their caresses tend to be inadequate. At least, that is what I had observed in women. Clint Verret did just the opposite: he pressed his fingers into my mouth, he allowed me to nibble and suck them. Still standing behind me, he placed his other hand on my neck and slid it down to my chest; he partially unbuttoned my shirt and crawled like a spider down to my belly. Suddenly he moved away. I got up from the chair and went toward him, but Verret pushed me, and there was the threat of a fight; he even threw a punch that stopped in midair. I grabbed him around the waist and he lowered his head; he said in the most serious, harshest voice I have ever heard in my life that he had never done it with a man. I responded, in the same kind of voice, that I hadn't either. "I swear I haven't," I added. And he asked: "And so?" Which was a little like asking: "Where do we begin?"

I unbuttoned his shirt and kissed him on the neck. I thought I heard him sob and I asked God not to let Verret break down just then; not to allow him to turn into a poor wretch filled with guilt and remorse. I didn't know exactly what I was looking for in him, but I was sure about what I didn't want. And I didn't want Verret acting like a little woman, ashamed, weepy, not even sweet. I wanted the more or less robust pianist I had met in the theater, and the grieving man, more or less an orphan, who struck me like lightning at breakfast. I wanted us to be men, lovers of Brahms, or lovers of any other composer; two inspired creatures who accede to music through a distinctive sensibility: that of desire.

Verret seemed to hear me—I don't know if I said, "God, don't fall apart"—I don't know if he understood the significance of the phrase that I pronounced in peremptory Spanish, as if it were an order. He took me by the shoulders and shook me before pushing me toward the bed. I feared for his hands, I trembled for his dear hands and tried to catch hold of them. Then I noticed that he was taller, whiter, more vengeful in the half-light, his contorted face panting uncontrollably over mine. Now I was the one who ran the risk of breaking down, of becoming weak and being rejected, of dissolving like a submissive, blushing little faggot. I realized that was the key: not to bend, not to cede, not to repent. We would learn—we learned—in the field. I offered myself with manliness. Something made me understand that, essentially, there was no other way to affirm than by moving forward. I offered myself first. I turned my back and understood that here lay true boldness. I felt pride—will anyone believe that I felt pride?—and I felt fiercer, more capable of loving, more invincible than I did with women. Verret came, he howled like an animal; he was very young and that wasn't enough by a long shot to weaken him. It was my turn and I also came, but more gently. Now no gesture, no tenderness, no gentleness could diminish my space. Now everything was permitted: I could caress his entire body, proceed as delicately as I wished. There is a beauty, a profound peace in lying with another man; a unique kind of tranquility never attained with a woman. I would not have wanted to die without experiencing it.

That night, as always, I went to the concert. I sat in the ninth row, taciturn and tired. My exhaustion was a feminine exhaustion—that is inevitable—and as I read the program notes I took delight in the pangs I felt: there are pains that redeem everything.

At exactly eight o'clock the musicians came out, the oboe sounded a perfect A, and the concertmaster echoed it. Two minutes later, followed by the conductor, Clint Verret appeared, handsome in his tails. His hair was pulled back in a knot. In bed, some hours earlier, he had loosened it, and his long reddish locks moved freely, covered my face, the ends stinging my eyes. Now his hair was shining, redder, smooth against his skull, the knot pulled taut. So much tautness gave him an air of cruelty, but even so I felt a rush of love.

I settled into my seat, and from that angle I could see his hands. My mind moved back and forth from Brahms to the small evocation of a gesture: Clint Verret's face, below my belly, looked up, exhausted, ready to move away. But then it inexplicably turned back and resumed the attack. That memory became sharper when the second movement, *Allegro appassionato,* began: nine and a half minutes of frenzy, Verret playing like a madman, enduring pangs as implacable as mine, and my wanting to fly to his side and cling to the shadowed whiteness of his back.

In those days I had often relished the sensation of watching the performance of a soloist whose body, hands, and mouth had been at the mercy of my hands, my unscrupulous lips. That complicity, combined with the music she was playing, always produced a state of euphoria in me. It was the euphoria of power, a mean-spirited joy, I cannot deny it: it told me I had possessed that body, and the hands that were playing, and the instrument, and if I chose I could spit on them or kiss them. A silent Guarnerius in the corner of the room witnesses my madness, but above all it witnesses the madness of the virtuosa who owns it. And I, who rise above both of them, possess them both; I possess the music they play, the shadow and the living cadence.

That sensation of seeing a soloist play whose body is so intensely mine was heightened and became almost unbearable as I listened to Verret. Fortunately he had reached the finale, the Hungarian reminiscences, the serene apotheosis, and the applause that woke us. Me and him, because Verret, too, was living a dream.

I could not even stand. I was perspiring for no real reason (it was cool in the auditorium); I loosened my tie and decided to follow Clint Verret to his next performance, in the city of Denver. At that moment, sitting in the middle of an audience that would not stop applauding, I realized that if I did not spend a few more days at his side, I never would really understand the rest. I never would completely understand this enigma of mine, much less forgive it.

For the moment, I thought only about putting my arms around Verret's waist, following him wherever I had to, stopping breathing with him, holding our breath together, and at the moment of collapse—the climax, which is a collapse—breathing in all the oxygen in the world, mouthful after mouthful, howl after howl. What passion can survive two hungry wolves?

When I went back to the dressing rooms, Verret was busy with a group of admirers, shaking hands, signing autographs. He threw me a glance, and I went to his side.

"I want you to come with me to Denver," he said very quietly.

I patted him on the back, a very manly gesture. I walked away from all that; I went out to the street and inhaled as if I were coming out of the water. As if the hand of God had pulled me up to the surface.

Virginia

I took her to the Hotel Pierre. The bar there is out of the way. I asked her what she wanted to drink. She asked for Coca-Cola and the world fell down around me.

"Wouldn't you like something stronger?"

She thought about it for a moment.

"Iced tea, perhaps." And she spoke to the waiter: "Bring me tea instead."

There was nothing I could do, and I despised her a little. Only a little, because at bottom I was impressed by her repertoire. I can't completely despise a musician who includes among her favorite pieces the violin sonatas of Béla Bartók (I could die when I hear them), and especially *Hora staccato* by Grigoras Dinicu, a difficult composition, but also perverse: beneath its dancing surface there is perversity. They brought the tea and she began to drink it in long swallows while I asked about her musical background. She spoke about her father the piano tuner, and her mother who ran away from Antigua. I thought that if I had been in her mother's place, I would have run away too; any woman who finds herself in the arms of a piano tuner who collects miniature violins has more than enough reason to run away. I've known a good number of piano tuners. Almost all of them are of a tortuous frame of mind; they have a somber way of approaching the piano and obsessing over the keyboard. A blind man used to come to the house to tune my daughter's piano. He wore enormous dark glasses and used a cane with little skulls carved into the handle. But what made me most uneasy were his hands—tiny, with the kind of gelatinous fingers that resemble embalmed worms. I never wanted to leave him alone with the girl. But I didn't like to leave him alone with the piano either. I don't know what I thought he was capable of. Almost everything, I suppose. There is arrogance, too, in piano tuners. In their heart of hearts, they are contemptuous of pianists.

"Forgive me for reacting the way I did," Virginia said suddenly, when I thought she would never broach the subject. "When you arrived, my brother had just left."

I had ordered whiskey and I was still in the dark. I took a sip and asked Virginia if her brother traveled with her.

"We never travel together," she answered in a low voice; she was in a kind of trance. "But he just arrived from Antigua and wants to go on with me to New York."

A brother, I thought. A cultivated, hermetic mulatto. Jealous to the marrow of his bones, and more aware than anyone of the defenselessness of this woman, the ingenuousness that was actually something else, a despicable resignation. Something made her vulnerable, that was true, but also violent: Virginia had to be very hard on herself. I didn't say a word, but she guessed what I was thinking.

"He lives part of the time in New York and part of the time in Antigua. He's older than I am and he has problems with Wendolyn, my secretary."

Wendolyn . . . Wendy to her friends, especially Virginia. It meant that the she-lion burning with desire had that clinging nickname so lacking in substance.

"I'm very sorry," I said, but I didn't want to ask any questions. I've realized over time that most women are likely to tell everything about their lives as long as they don't notice excessive interest in the other person. I've learned to be a distant interlocutor. At times I might even seem rude.

"I'd like to stay here," Virginia said suddenly. "Rent a room for me."

She opened her bag and took out her passport, but I stopped her.

"I'll rent it in my name."

Her face was slightly swollen. Because of that, and the bruise on her jaw, I had no doubt she had been hit. I finished my drink and in my mind I saw the image of her body in underwear, her back turned, the rest of the room in disorder. I didn't know if I should ask what her plans were. Virginia was lost in thought; perhaps she was involved in making them. For the moment, she could stay at the Pierre for one or two nights. Call her agent in New York and cancel the performance. Avoid any contact with Wendolyn, a hyperactive and unfortunate she-lion. And, above all, avoid any kind of meeting with her brother, who was not hyperactive but just the opposite: a sullen, slow-moving man—in this he resembled Virginia some-what—with well-tended hands (I'm referring to those long, mulatto hands with extremely clean nails painted with colorless polish).

"Wait here for me," I whispered, and I caressed her shoulder in a friendly way.

I took a room. The clerks at the Pierre know me. I've used the hotel with other virtuosas. Soloists traveling with a relative who can't use their own rooms. Virginia waited for me at the bar. She didn't show much emotion; she didn't even allow herself a moment's hesitation when I suggested we go up together. Sometimes the same musicians who impose on themselves a difficult schedule of ten or twelve hours of practice a day turn into stupidly obedient creatures, so docile that I occasionally have found it irritating. They emerge like zombies from the steam bath of their studios—and I'm referring not to the temperature of the room but to the musical bonfire—and they are damp, inside and out. It is so easy to take them then. . . . Nobody can imagine how simple it is to look into their eyes, put an arm around their shoulders, and push them gently toward the street. From there to the hotel is no more than a step. Generally they are exhausted, their mind and their arms can do no more—if she's a clarinetist you have to be careful, very careful of her lips—but the rest of the body, and all its desires, are intact. They maintain the fire; in fact, the musical climax makes them want to achieve the other climax: they are burning up inside. Most of the time they don't realize that as they practice the violin—persistent about their staccato—or repeat the same piece over and over again on the piano, they are also on their way to perdition. After that, there is no more noble service to fine music, no more imperishable support one can offer a soloist, than to throw her facedown on a bed. There they finally explode. All the feeling that has been accumulating for hours—sometimes days—erupts in a dazzling, almost animal outburst. Cellists howl more than the others. And almost all of them tend to be wildly passionate, or too demanding.

None of the desk clerks looked up when I walked past them on my way to the elevators, holding Virginia Tuten's arm. Her elbow was fleshy; I pressed it intentionally: I wanted her to feel secure, in a sense to accept me as another protective brother. Since she had no luggage, I offered to go with her to buy clothes, or to pick up what she had left at the other hotel.

"I don't want to go back there," she whispered. "At least for today, I want to forget all about it."

She dropped into an armchair and I turned on the lights. Night was falling and I understood that Virginia had begun to collapse; she was becoming aware of everything that had happened and what still needed to be done: canceling a concert, with only a few hours advance notice, was a very serious and dangerous decision.

"Are you sure you don't want to play?" I asked, squatting in front of her.

"I didn't say that," she replied, not looking at me.

"But by now," I insisted, "you ought to be leaving for the theater."

"My brother will be there, waiting for me. I won't be able to play if I sense him close by."

I took her hands, hands that were incredibly delicate, considering her voluptuous mulatta's body. I kissed them; I was trying to measure my steps, but I imagined that those damp, brief, in a certain sense disinterested little kisses would not disturb her too much. Suddenly I realized my error: they *were* disturbing her. Virginia had been too long at the mercy of another woman, I mean, without the roughness of a man. I thought that Wendolyn, the disagreeable she-lion, had just lost her; she would go on losing her as the night advanced, and by dawn not even a trace of her memory would remain. It didn't matter that in the future she would continue to coordinate interviews, attend to the violinist's wardrobe, her scores, her airplane tickets; it didn't matter that she would continue to confront her brother, that incestuous, despicable mulatto. Wendy, from that day on, was excluded; we were meticulously excluding her.

As I kissed her hands, Virginia passed her fingers over my lips and along my mustache, she caressed my cheekbones, my temples, my hair, which in those days was wavy and black, perhaps only dark brown, but fragrant and thick. Suddenly, I sensed that I ought to pause. I stood and explained that I had to go to the paper, and in the meantime she could make her calls. I promised I'd be back in a couple of hours, and before I left I took her by the chin and kissed her on the mouth.

I dashed to my house. At that time it was relatively easy for me to invent a trip out of the city, a concert I had forgotten about completely. Along with the concert, I invented a supper and a gathering afterward, and with all that going on I would have to stay in a hotel, there was no help for it. My wife took it philosophically; sometimes she insisted she wanted to go with me, and then I would convince her that it would be a difficult trip and the soloist wasn't worth the bother. Inexplicably, she would agree. Now, many years later, I have thought that she offered to accompany me knowing ahead of time that I would try to dissuade her. I suppose she took advantage of those nights of freedom to live her own life. I have two or three well-founded suspicions: a colleague of hers, also a lawyer; the ear, nose, and throat specialist who took care of my daughter; and, of course, one of the private detectives she would hire, in the name of her clients, to follow adulterous husbands.

I changed my clothes and called the paper. The photographer had returned to the editorial offices in a fury without seeing me or the violinist. I asked them to explain to him that the virtuosa had suddenly fallen ill. I promised to send them a report as soon as I had more details. I patted on a discreet cologne, adjusted the knot of my tie, and said good-bye to my daughter, not without first asking her to practice hard. I also said good-bye to my wife: I'm affectionate by nature. I gave her a long kiss and reminded her that I loved her.

I arrived at the Pierre and went directly to the elevator. Since I was alone, one of the clerks stopped me to say hello and ask me something about a singer, a successful bolero singer, I seem to recall. Even in those days boleros irritated me, and people who sang them irritated me even more. But I answered pleasantly and in detail, like the connoisseur he thought I was. Then I went up to the room. I knocked gently at the door; I had the key but preferred to knock so as not to startle Virginia. She didn't answer. I used my key and walked into the shadows. She had closed the windows, and everything was quiet except for the sound of running water, which was turned on full force; I supposed she was bathing.

I removed my jacket and took a deep breath. I pushed open the door and the image shook me: Virginia was in the tub and had fainted (or had pretended to), though her head was out of the water. I turned off the faucet and took her in my arms; she was naked but warm. The water too was warm; at least she had taken the trouble to make it warm. She babbled something; I blew in her face and whispered that we would go to bed. She opened her eyes, enclosed me in her arms, and made my shirt soaking wet.

Biting my ear, she begged me to take her far away.

"Sᴇʙᴀsᴛɪᴀ́ɴ, are you awake?"

"I'm dreaming, Agustín. . . . Can I dream about Verret?"

"You can, Sebastián, but you shouldn't. Look, when he played very open chords, Verret's hands looked like two octopuses; he could extend his fingers from here to here."

"Two freckled octopuses."

"Exactly. Two magnificent octopuses."

"Where does Verret live, Agustín?"

"Who knows? He was in Brazil for a while—he lived there with somebody for a few months—but he must have returned to Sydney. Are you going back to sleep?"

"That depends. If you bring me something to read, I'll take off my mask."

"Well, then take it off, you madman. I'll leave these pages here for you. . . . Are you sure you're awake?"

Alejandrina

THE HARPSICHORD, the piano, and the celeste. Impossible to conceive of a more complete angel. Alejandrina Sanromá came into my life—I mean, she passed through my life—during one of those periods of drought when I thought I would never again go mad with passion. I obsessed over this idea in the same way that some writers obsess over the blank page. I was blank; the world around me was blank too. I came to believe that my last relationship, a hideous affair with the violinist Manuela Suggia, had made me incapable of ever feeling again. The last descent into hell that we undertook together occurred early in June. Suddenly it was November, I had endured months of enforced fidelity, and faced with my sadness, my wandering through the house like a soul in torment, my wife became terrified: she thought I was planning to leave her. For the first time I noticed that she was suspicious when I went out; she would look through my pockets, spy on me when I talked on the phone. How could I explain to her that I had never been so faithful for so long or with so much intensity?

I was empty, and for that reason it didn't even occur to me to look at another woman. I went so far as to wonder if I had fallen in love with Manuela, a depraved blood-sucker, if I had been trapped in her memory, her violent acrimony at the end. I was hit hard by depression, a sense of hopelessness that seemed to drain out through my pores. I would wake up in the middle of the night, suffocating in my bed, but forcing myself to stay there, waiting for the light of dawn that filtered in gradually and changed color minute by minute. Toward daybreak my wife would begin to snore; the only snoring that has always filled me with tenderness has been hers. With my lovers it was different. Their snoring amused or annoyed me, or even moved me to pity, and on occasion it was the sign that told me it was time to leave.

As it turned out, Alejandra Sanromá never snored. Or at least, I didn't hear her snore because we never slept together. We spent a few nights wide awake, and had several afternoons of tropical siestas when neither of us fell asleep. She was an uneasy angel, and for that very reason she was always on the alert, hanging on my slightest gesture, her hallucinatory eyes feverish, seeming to forgive my retaliation. Because with her I wanted to retaliate.

She joined the orchestra when the regular pianist became ill. I've already said that it was November, the end of November, and that other odious month was upon us: sheer cruelty far removed from April's. I went to the theater unwillingly; I didn't expect much from those slovenly musicians who rehearsed in shorts and tee shirts. In the midst of my dejection I realized that we were growing old together: the brasses and I, the concertmaster and I, the organist—years ago she and I had enjoyed a brief flirtation—and I. The quality of the music varied, depending on the conductor who mounted the podium. I was beginning to know it all by heart, and there was no mistake or slip that I could not anticipate: the tubas losing their way, the harp stumbling, the occasional lack of control in the strings' attack.

I sat in the ninth row, toward the left. As soon as I sat down, I was filled with a desire to leave. What I liked best about rehearsals, the empty theater, oppressed me so much this time that I made an impatient gesture and my notebook fell to the floor. A notebook full of nonsense, as empty as everything else around me. At that moment the soloist walked out, a short, taciturn trumpeter getting ready to rehearse Hummel's Concerto. I listened without blinking: he had expressive talent and a rare imagination, but I concentrated on his body. I saw that he was suffering—or enjoying—a slight erection as he performed a passage from the second movement. Some very temperamental male soloists react like hanged men: they become excited and cannot control themselves. At rehearsals it is more apparent because they are dressed carelessly; they don't wear a jacket, they have on summer trousers. Cellists and pianists, because they are seated, can conceal it successfully. It is more difficult for a violinist, and for a trumpet player it must be almost impossible: they thrust out their bellies like Arabic dancers, and the movements demanded by the trumpet propel them into lust.

Now that I'm recalling the trumpeter, I think it's too bad I didn't like men more. Clint Verret was my most sincere passion. There was also a violist; he liked to call himself the violated violist. But at heart he was a worm. When we had finished, he was overcome by guilt, he complained of nausea, he called his wife from the bed. The sheets were very stained. "They're so dirty," I remember his saying to me. "You're so contemptible," I remember answering.

As soon as they finished rehearsing the trumpet concerto, the conductor told the musicians that they would continue with *The Planets*; I've always had contradictory feelings about the piece. I like the themes of Mars and Jupiter, for example, but despise the one for Neptune. Gustav Holst, the man who composed the suite, was a superstitious arthritic, mad about astral charts and Chinese horoscopes, and I'll bet that in all that cabbala some dark hidden desire throbbed behind the stardust. I picked up the notebook from the floor and couldn't decide whether to stay a little longer in the theater or finally leave, which I had been wanting to do. Then I happened to glance at one end of the stage, where two men were setting up the celeste next to the organ. A woman came out to supervise the placement of the instrument: her hair was very short, almost flat against her skull; her eyes were enormous, but not protruding, simply wide open, unforgivably open and black. She sat down at the celeste and made a comment to the organist. A light suddenly came on in my head; I stood and walked to the third row, which is where Salieri usually sat. I don't know why they called him that; I don't even know what his real name was. Salieri, an obese music lover, attended orchestra rehearsals for more than thirty years until he died. He knew the musicians by first name and last; he had personal information about almost all of them: marriages, number of children, spousal desertions, the approximate date of their retirement. He was a meek creature with the head of an ox, and was allowed to attend rehearsals because of his willingness to be useful—he brought coffee, carried instruments—and his constant flattery of the bassists. Poor Salieri suspected what I had known since I first approached the orchestra: whoever wants to win the sympathy of those musicians has to begin by buttering up the basses. They, more than the violins, exercise a great influence over the entire company, a secret but very efficient command.

When I sat down beside him, Salieri looked at me out of the corner of his eye.

"The woman at the celeste," I asked straight out, "is she new?"

He cleared his throat and pretended he hadn't heard me. I waited a few seconds and leaned toward him.

"She hasn't played before, or has she?"

Salieri adjusted his glasses; he was heavy and phlegmatic. He moved his neck with difficulty, like an old mechanical doll, and gave me a rancorous look. It was evident that I could not enter his kingdom. On occasion I had dared to criticize the orchestra, the bassists of his heart, and, of course, the trombones.

"Teresa has the flu," he said very quietly, referring to the orchestra's regular pianist. "They called Alejandrina Sanromá to replace her."

I made note of her name. Salieri was a very useful maniac, but I didn't dare ask him anything else. I returned to my seat in the ninth row and began to recover my hope. Perhaps I should not define it this way. I began to recover my balance, the longing that is indispensable to my equilibrium, and I must confess that this equilibrium centered on my passion for women who had mastered an instrument.

I listened to Holst's work as if I myself were whirling around a ball of light. The notes coming out of the celeste mimicked the stardust left behind in Mercury's wake. I was following Alejandrina's movements, the way she looked at the conductor, her initial nervousness. One's first time with an orchestra is always intimidating. The conductor, who was Romanian, upbraided the musicians in Spanish and English; he was demanding a pianissimo that the violas couldn't give him. Suddenly he ordered everyone to be quiet and said, stressing each syllable, "If you can hear it, it's not pianissimo." Alejandra smiled when she heard this; it was the smile that convinced me.

When the rehearsal was over, I looked for her backstage. I found her standing next to the harpsichord; certainly she played the harpsichord too. It was the first thing I asked her, even before I introduced myself. She said she did, of course, but preferred the piano, and especially the celeste. I tried out the asexual expression of a sentimental critic: I said I adored the tinkling bell sound the instrument produces, and had ever since I saw the *Nutcracker* for the first time, when I was four or five years old.

"The same thing happened to me," responded Alejandrina, taking the bait.

I added that it had just occurred to me that it would be a nice idea to write an article for children, telling them about the celeste and the harpsichord. And no doubt the best way to do it would be to interview her.

Alejandrina Sanromá accepted with enthusiasm. I asked her when. She said that very night. I asked her to have supper with me and she made a coquettish gesture that sealed her fate: "I'll have to go home and change."

I smiled at her. In my head another celeste was beginning its depraved tinkling.

"If you don't mind, I'll go home with you and wait."

It was an audacious move, but it worked. She lived very close to the theater and we walked to her building. Her apartment was on the ninth floor, a number that has always brought me good luck; she lived there with her adolescent daughter. The girl—small joys that the planets provide to us—was spending some time with her father. Alejandrina was an overripe fruit; you could smell her desire for combat from a mile away. As we were walking she remarked that she always read my reviews. I denied their importance, pretended to be humble, preferred to concentrate on the questions I was asking her. I tried to confuse her and flatter her at the same time. I confused her by keeping my distance, maintaining a journalistic attitude. Soon after we entered the apartment she excused herself, went to change her clothes, and left me alone in the living room. A few moments earlier she had offered me a glass of wine, put on a record of pieces for celeste—always so libidinous—and given me a catalogue to look at of celestes manufactured in England. My good angel did not have a celeste of her own because they were too expensive. But she did have a very respectable upright piano. I thought I would ask her to play something, but then I had a better idea.

She reappeared a few minutes later. She had put on a rather demure black dress with long sleeves and a nun's neckline. I know from experience that this kind of steep obstacle very often signifies just the opposite. I looked at her from head to toe and stood up: it was time for us to go. On the way I suggested that we stop at the conservatory. I thought it was the only place where I could find a celeste. The one in the theater would do me no good; I couldn't get backstage at this time of night, least of all with a woman. At the conservatory, however, the night watchmen knew me; they were accustomed to seeing me at night. From time to time I would go there to prepare my classes or write my reviews.

The celeste was in the studio of the piano instructor. I asked God not to let the key be turned. And it wasn't. We went in and I switched on the light, which seemed oppressive, so white and liquid. I looked around for a small lamp and saw one on the desk, next to the bookcase. I turned that one on and immediately turned off the ceiling light. Alejandrina had gone over to the celeste; she caressed it with her fingertips. Suddenly she began to use the intimate *tú* with me:

"If you write that article, don't forget to say that the celeste has only one pedal."

It seemed idiotic but I agreed, and asked her to play something. She settled herself on the bench, and I heard the first chords.

"Tchaikovsky," I purred, recognizing the melody. "His nephew was fascinated by the celeste."

Alejandrina raised her head and looked into my eyes. That was enough. Then she concentrated again on the keyboard and I concentrated on the strategic possibilities of the studio: there wasn't a damn sofa where I could lay her down, not even a reasonable armchair. There weren't even any rugs.

"That young man used to sit next to Tchaikovsky," I said hesitantly, as if coming out with a gem, "and insist on playing with his uncle."

"Celeste for four hands?" Alejandrina smiled. "That must be uncomfortable."

I put on a look of surprise. The wet little angel trying to be sarcastic with her guardian devil.

"Tchaikovsky would get furious," I lied slowly, not actually sure I was lying, "but he only pretended to be angry, because in his heart of hearts he liked being close to his nephew. He tussled with him, growled like a wolf, sniffed at his cold little ears. . . . That was how he composed *The Dance of the Sugarplum Fairy*."

Alejandrina looked at me with suspicion. She had Oriental lips, the kind of small, carefully painted mouth that I suddenly intended to devour.

"Not his ears exactly," I corrected myself, "but behind his ears. There's a place there . . ."

She pretended not to hear me and I took her hand; for a moment I took possession of her cold little fingers, snatched them away from the celeste and rubbed them against my lips. It was as if I had whispered magic words, because her entire hand seemed to recover all its strength; it became completely independent and began to caress me. First my chest and then one of my thighs; finally it took refuge in my crotch. There it could capture everything; it captured my passion, fully reinvigorated, and it captured something that is called instinct. That's always in the testicles.

"We'd better go," she murmured without releasing me, without her body's showing the slightest intention of moving.

I obliged her to stand and I kissed her. I went to the desk and turned off the lamp. In complete darkness I came back and began to undress her: black falling on black. We couldn't see each other; I heard only her breathing and noticed her hands unfastening my trousers. I finished undressing her by touch and asked her to return to the celeste. She sat down with difficulty, stifling her laughter, stumbling a little. When she was seated on the bench, I approached her from behind and leaned against her back, took her breasts in both hands, and began to kiss her shoulders. A short while later I whispered into her ear:

"Play something."

I heard a very soft "No." She stammered that she couldn't.

"Not even that part of *Salome* . . . ?"

She rubbed her face against mine.

"That least of all."

Licking the nape of the neck of a woman about to play the celeste must be the closing chord of madness, not the opening one. I realized that everything could be ruined at any moment: all she had to do was turn and embrace me, something so conventional after all; or I, surrendering to derangement, could seize her around the waist and pull her down to the floor.

"Then play something else," I moaned. "Play whatever you want."

She began to laugh, but without conviction.

"The Dance of the Sugarplum Queen," she murmured.

"Not queen," I corrected, "fairy."

She began to play, somewhat tentatively at first, as if just awaking, but with more spirit as she became con-vinced of the sweet reward that awaited her at the end. I kneeled behind the bench and kissed her back, making each little kiss coincide with the notes of the tinkling bells: C C C, B B B, A A A, $F^\#A$ G A $F^\#$. With my arms around her naked body, panting in the darkness of that studio, I felt the return of the emotion that I thought had been exhausted with Manuela. Finally it became a challenge for Alejandrina to go on playing while I caressed her. And that, in short, was the real secret of the melody: a perverse wolf wrapped in cotton candy.

I stood and she stopped playing. It was difficult to orient oneself in the darkness, and it was delicious to find a clue: a breast, a thigh, Alejandrina's lips desperate to trap my sex, and eventually succeeding. She applied herself then; that's a good thing about virtuosas: they apply themselves, they insist, they repeat, they possess a thirst for perfection that knows neither boredom nor exhaustion.

Without waiting for the denouement, I gently withdrew from her mouth and obliged her to move away slightly from the celeste.

"Lean back," I whispered, and she understood immediately.

I kneeled in front of her and asked her to extend her

hands; I only wanted to know if she could reach the keyboard.

"Now," I sobbed, "can you play?"

She leaned her body forward; only the tips of her buttocks rested on the bench, and I, sitting on the floor, buried my head between her thighs.

" 'The Dance . . . ,' " she sighed, "shall I play it again?"

The sugarplum, all the honey in the world, was there beneath my tongue, and the hands of Alejandrina Sanromá played despite my voracity, but also despite her madness. She had gone mad, and from Tchaikovsky she leaped to some other piece I could not identify. The sound of her moans combined with the tinkling bells of the celeste, and at the moment I felt her coming, I heard her bang the instrument, beat on it furiously. Alejandrina stopped playing and with drawn-out sobs she put her hands on my head—on my face of a sugarplummed goblin—and gradually calmed down.

I sat up and sucked her nipples. I no longer cared that there was no sofa, not even an armchair, in the studio. I pushed her gently to the floor and lay on top of her. I had never had so slender a body under mine; I thought I didn't

like bony women. But I was wrong. Alejandrina's bones
pushed against my bones, especially around the hips, and
the painful sensation it produced filled me with macabre
pleasure: we were two skeletons beating each other to
death, trying to break against the other, striking to see
which of us would come apart first.

I raised Alejandrina's legs and held them up with my
hands before brutally entering her. That would be the
final thrust, the coup de grâce for a little piece of flesh
that, touched by the fairy wand, was about to turn into
luminous dust. Alejandrina shrieked, and if I didn't shriek
with the same intensity it was because I was overwhelmed
by the joy of having recovered my passion, which is nothing but the feeling of being born and dying in a single second, and being reborn knowing that now nothing can kill
you.

I was immortal, practically invincible when I withdrew
from Alejandrina Sanromá's body. I stumbled against the
celeste before I could reach the desk in order to turn on
the lamp. Alejandrina lay motionless on the floor, and I
searched my clothes for a handkerchief. I went back to her
and dried her crotch as if I were wiping away tears.

We dressed and went to supper. Alejandrina did not drink a drop of liquor—she never drank—but she seemed intoxicated. She asked me to come home with her and I warned her that she would regret it. I warned her with a certain guile, and she replied that she didn't care. The only thing she wanted that night was to regret everything, be impatient for everything, weep with her desire to weep. She wanted me to take her right side up and inside out, nicely and nice and rough, suddenly, without warning, without mercy. I turned red; I had never known a pianist, virtuosa or not, so brazen in her speech. Alejandrina ranted in a quiet voice, but even so I thought that someone at a nearby table might hear her. We had dessert and I confessed that I liked her very much. She trembled inside her black dress: a blackness as overwhelming and bewitching as the coursing of her own blood.

When Saturday came I attended the concert, as always. From the stage, before she sat down at the celeste, Alejandrina looked for me. I had said that I would be in the ninth row, toward the left. She smiled when she saw me and I was afraid she would throw me a kiss or play a passage from *The Dance of the Sugarplum Fairy*: I knew she was capable of going to any extreme. I felt at ease only when she had finished her part in *The Planets*, a suite that had never seemed so long or so flagrant in its vulgar lewdness.

Two months later I went mad again, but this time my beloved played the clarinet. Rebecca Cheng, aside from being almost a child, was an experienced acrobat. My irrepressible Chinese girl and I attempted unnatural positions and caresses worthy of circus performers. There was no need to have recourse to ignominy, as with Manuela Suggia.

Rebecca laughed at almost everything. She had the laugh of an astute little Chinese girl caught stealing a lotus blossom from someone else's pond.

Virginia

IN REALITY, Virginia Tuten's brother wasn't her brother but her cousin. Her father the piano tuner had legally adopted the boy when Virginia was only a few months old, and they grew up together in the family home in Antigua. And often slept together until Virginia turned fourteen and her father sent her to study in New York.

She told me the story, sobbing, following a rather dull body-to-body encounter. We were still lying side by side, somewhat disoriented, and I listened to her in silence, barely able to decipher her hoarse whispering. Virginia talked about the street where she had grown up; about the games she used to play after practicing the violin five or six hours a day; about the woman—a painter with only one arm—who reared her and replaced her mother. It was that woman who caught them, Virginia and her adoptive brother, stuck together as if playing a game while they watched television. That was when they sent her away from Antigua.

I listened to all this while I caressed her belly; I rubbed it slowly as if I wanted to relieve a pain. After the initial shock of finding her half-fainting in the bathtub, I realized, because I know too many violinists, that Virginia was looking for attention, but I realized above all that she was a classic case of a poorly loved virtuosa. The intention of her performance was to frighten me, and since all fright activates a small dose of lust, to take advantage of this and thoroughly seduce me.

After I took her out of the water, while I was wrapping her in towels, she watched me out of the corner of her eye and lucidly scrutinized my reactions. She was a very bad actress, Virginia Tuten. All her talent, all her intelligence lay in how she played; in the mournful audacity, for example, that she would bring to the *Moderato nobile* of the Korngold Concerto (although I didn't know it then; I listened to her play it much later). She wasn't even a good lover. I've already said that the body-to-body had been very dull. But in that dullness, in the way we hurried and then sank into a kind of lethargy, was the germ of a greater problem. I fell in love like an imbecile with Virginia Tuten, and I fell in love for a reason that I still, at my age and with the wisdom time has given me, cannot explain. She was not the most beautiful, or the most amusing, or the most inspired of my virtuosas. She did not teach me anything special about the violin, those small moments of enlightenment that would arise with other soloists when, in order to please me, they would play a portion of some concerto, naked, in front of me. Virginia too often took refuge on her cloud; she would hide in a corner like a sick dog. She lacked enthusiasm—not so much for the violin as for life—and my knowing that she was so unfathomable may have swayed my feelings. Because I could not reach her, she became, in my eyes, a helpless creature, a wild but at the same time a very sad animal.

Physically I liked her very much. I say "very much" and yet I think about her defects: her too-wide hips, the morbid texture of her belly; she was heavy through the thighs and backside, like a good mulatta; her feet were as big as a man's, and she used straighteners on her hair: the kinks were tamed and smoothed, but still coarse. Once when we were at rest—it was as insipid as the battle—I asked if she too had the "mark of Saint-Saëns." She emerged from her stupor to look at me and reply that she had no idea what that was.

"It's a mark that some violinists have," I said very quietly, indicating the place on my own neck.

"Nonsense," she exclaimed, "I don't know anybody who has one."

I sat up in bed to tell her about the Chinese violinist and the thick maroon-colored line he had on the left side above the collarbone. I cited the example of clarinetists. Kissing one of them can be delicious: they tend to have a little callus on the lower lip, on the inside, and that little callus can irritate another person's lips. Irritate or incite, depending on who feels it: it excited me no end. I don't know if that was the best example, but at least it achieved the effect I wanted. Virginia turned over with some effort, it seemed to me; lying on her back, she looked as wide as a sea lion.

"Well, I don't have any mark," she said, presenting herself to me. "You can check if you want."

I had to admit it was true as I kissed her neck: immaculate on both sides. That was enough to make me want to massacre it, suck it fiercely and leave behind not the "mark of Saint-Saëns" but my own stubborn, damp imprint.

"You ought to come to New York with me," she said into my ear; it was obvious she had been thinking about it for some time.

I ignored her remark. I couldn't tell her what she probably already suspected: I was married to a very enthusiastic woman who did not demand either large or small sacrifices from me; I had a daughter with a good ear for music—not the virtuosa she was, of course, but disciplined. Besides, I enjoyed my work at the conservatory, and especially liked writing interviews and reviews for the paper.

"Wendolyn will come to an agreement with my brother," she added, referring to the desirous she-lion, "and between the two of them they'll get me out of here. I know what's going to happen: they'd rather see me dead."

She had a fondness for melodrama. But even this sickening trait, which has always irritated me so much in both men and women, I could excuse in her.

"I don't recognize them anymore," she insisted. "I don't know who my brother is or who my secretary is. My life has become a calamity."

Egocentric, too, like almost all the strings (cellists tend to be even worse), the world revolved around her tiny world. I remained silent and she curled up beside me. The first impression that I'd had at the theater was reaffirmed in that intimacy: Virginia was a sinful wet nurse; she had the most enormous tits I'd ever seen. The tits of a generous black woman who nursed her own babies, of course, but also the white baby, the one who is the outsider and yet sucks the most. I became a baby, I became a beggar at her breast, which suddenly was transformed into a kind of womb closed to any kind of judgment, denied to any kind of enigma other than that of desire. I squeezed my eyes shut so that I would be blind, and I began the journey in reverse, naked for the first time: I entered her with desire and came into her womb. Then I prayed that nothing and no one would ever bring me back into the world.

On that second tour of her body, I was more aware that in the slowness and silence, in the supposed indifference with which Virginia received me, I found a stimulus that I hadn't found in other women. She wasn't a good lover, that's true. Virginia was something else, and possessing her was in another category. Like possessing something that isn't human—a stone perhaps, or an animal. At that level, drowsing in her flesh, enjoying that calm, I can swear that I went crazy. I've never reached what I reached with Virginia with any other woman. On no other sex did I spend so many hours of self-sacrificing tongue. And I meditated on no other relationship with so much urgency, so much fear. I died for her, I melted when I heard her play, and for the first time in many years I felt that my marriage was foundering.

"Fat idiot violinist," I murmured months later, in the hotel in New York where we met. Virginia was naked and playing with her back to me. My whim had been for her to perform that piece, *Hora staccato*, an ominous, provocative melody that had come from the brain of a depressed Romanian. Virginia's whim was to play it naked, at the window, but with her back to me. When she finished and turned around to look at me, she saw the spectacle that confirmed my ruin for her: I was a whipped grotesque who could not endure the sight of her flesh without surrendering his will, or without suffering the most peremptory, violet-colored, desperate erections. I was crying like a baby, with desire and love.

"Come here," I remember saying to her, giving a laughable order to the absolute mistress of all orders.

"You come," Virginia shouted, still holding the violin in one hand and the bow in the other.

She turned around and faced the window again. I walked toward her and stopped close to her, the distance necessary to smell her odor, similar to the scent of nutmeg, but mixed with the fragrance of her breasts, which was an original aroma. Still floating in the air was the diabolical tempo of the Romanian melody, and I understood that I couldn't take another step. At that moment I couldn't touch her, or fall on my knees and bite her buttocks, or spread her legs and dive in from below, like a calf feeding on her sex, something I had done so often. If I embraced her I could explode inside and collapse. In a second I could die.

She glanced at me and smiled. Then she placed the instrument on her shoulder again and began to play. It was the *Valse triste*, by the madman Nerval, that fatuous, funereal music.

How could she be so implacably a bitch?

"I FEEL LIKE one of those very old Eskimos," said Sebastián. "Somebody else chews his food for him and puts the pap in his mouth."

I didn't respond. He sat down across from me and I became depressed thinking that both of us really were ready for pap.

"I say this because of your memoirs, or stories, or whatever they are. You're giving them to me prechewed, which is convenient for you, of course. What we have now is a nice little romance novel."

I smiled without wanting to, just to revive his spirits, and I went on reviewing my notes: loose sheets, grimy notebooks, date books from years long past, too long past and too vivid. The rest was in my memory, the only thing that would not fail me at that moment of slow, visceral foundering.

"You haven't told me if you finally went to Denver with Clint Verret," Sebastián added, and at the same time he fixed me with a suffering look, a look as suppliant as a mother's.

I barricaded myself behind cruelty. I warned him that envy was consuming him, and that at his age, which was almost the same as mine, he had to learn to control himself.

"You must know that I'm sick of your romance with the moronic mulatta," I heard him murmur. "How did you have the stomach to put up with her for so long?"

"It was, in fact, a part of my stomach that she stole," I said emphatically, not looking at him. "According to the Berbers, the liver is the seat of love. And you give your liver when you fall in love."

Sebastián made a gesture of disbelief and returned the pages I had given him the day before. In them I spoke about Virginia, about my true feelings for that woman. I had never confessed them to anyone. Perhaps not even to myself.

"In the end," he said ironically, "she had to go back to New York with her dyke secretary and her dear, sweet brother."

"He wasn't her brother," I corrected him.

"I know, her adoptive brother, her cousin . . . whatever."

"He was her husband, Sebastián. I found out when I was in New York, don't ask me how. Virginia was a machine for fabricating lies."

For an instant Sebastián dropped his resentful attitude and laughed out loud.

"She was exactly like you; that's what charmed you."

"That wasn't it," I answered, my voice trembling, betraying that the opposite was true.

Then I began to read a press release that somebody had left on my desk. I read it with a mixture of nostalgia and panic: the pianist Margarita Shevchenko was appearing in San Juan this weekend. It was going to be the first concert I would attend without a concrete purpose: I didn't have to write the review, and I no longer had students to whom I would recommend the performance and then discuss it with them in class. I didn't even have the incentive of seducing the pianist, regardless of the tumultuous Shevchenko's appearance. From now on music would be nothing more than the peaceful oasis sentimentalists say it is. It never was that for me. But now, facing a future without passion, I had to find its raison d'être; I needed to confront that reality like someone who crosses a frontier and then feels himself all over to see if he's whole, to make sure he hasn't lost an arm or gotten a hole in his belly. I had to attend that concert, preferably alone—no wife, no sympathetic friends—and leave there knowing that all my emotion, that indigestible lump of sentiments and revelations, had to be left somewhere, but never again at the paper. I had to take it home with me and not do anything with it. Go on living, which is all you can do at my age.

Sebastián stopped complaining about what I had written to talk to one of his reporters, who came in with a news item about a divorce—of a famous actress, I thought I heard. Then the editorial offices became quiet again. Sebastián announced that he would go back to his desk and let me write.

"Just one thing," he added. "How does that little number on the celeste end?"

I looked him up and down. He finally had succeeded in irritating me.

"What do you mean how does it end? It's ended. Didn't you realize that? Some things end happily."

"You're right. Now you need to tell me how it ended with Verret. I hope it had a sad ending; that's the kind of story I like."

"It ended in Denver," I whispered, doling out the information in small bits.

"So quickly?"

"We spent three days in the Brown Palace. What we had there is worth twenty years of moderate cohabitation."

"You didn't go out?"

Sebastián had turned slightly pale; he was swallowing urgently, his mouth dry.

"The interior of that hotel is like an old-fashioned ship, with bronze balustrades and galleries. I pretended I was at sea."

Sebastián half-closed his eyes. He made a gesture as if he had suffered a dizzy spell—pure theater—and completely abandoned his caustic tone.

"Then write it, Agustín. I was looking in the morgue for photographs of Verret. I took out one; I have it on my desk if you want to see it."

I refused vehemently, as if he had suggested a suicide pact. Something in my reencounter with the image of the pianist had terrified me. I didn't fall in love with Verret because I don't fall in love with men. That had been clear from the beginning.

"If you'll permit me," I said, "I'll finish the story of Virginia Tuten and then I'll write about Rebecca Cheng. Rebecca's story is amusing."

"Verret!" Sebastián cut me off; his distress moved me. "First tell me about Verret and then you can go on with the mulatta, with the Chinese girl, with any woman you like."

I saw that he was perspiring and that his hands were trembling slightly. I stood, put my face close to his, stared into his eyes, the tip of my nose almost touching his, like one of those ferocious sergeants trying to intimidate a recruit. I bit off each word as I spoke.

"What happens if I tell you another little romance novel, Sebastián?"

He was dumbfounded. He hesitated before asking: "Who was the romance with?"

"With Verret. Suppose I tell you that the bastard was another one who stole part of my liver?"

His imagination was about to explode. More than the heart, more than the head, there is an organ of mad dreams, and it always explodes through the eyes.

"You and Verret . . ." Sebastián stammered.

"I'm no faggot," I thundered in a whisper.

"But Verret . . ."

"Neither was he. And still he stole my liver. Can you explain that?"

He nodded yes and walked away slowly. I felt sorry for him. I wanted to call Verret, to find him in the farthest corner of Australia, under the rocks, in the stinking pouches of kangaroos. I swallowed with a dry mouth too: how far would I go in my attempt to tell everything? How much was I going to risk?

I closed my eyes and seemed to hear a passage from Hiller's étude for piano. I saw lights and glasses, and the unforgettable balconies of the Brown Palace whirling around me. Verret's voice came to me so clearly:

"Brown is the color of the lie."

Without our touching each other, I felt that we had embraced. We were two gentlemen standing on deck and looking out at the ocean. And that, perhaps, was the only truth.

Verret

I ARRIVED IN Denver with just enough time to drop off my suitcase, change my clothes, and go to the rehearsal with Verret. We were in separate rooms, naturally, but I did everything possible to arrange for us to be on the same floor. The hotel was called the Brown Palace, and it really was palatial. Inside, it reminded me of ships in the movies, those luxurious ocean liners on which the music is played by string quartets.

Verret had arrived the day before. He had to take care of some business related to his contract, and we preferred to delay our encounter a little: it would have been excessive if we had left San Juan together and arrived at the hotel in Denver together.

Ferdinand Hiller was constantly floating between us. To me he had always seemed a composer heavily influenced by his friends, Mendelssohn and Schumann. Verret thought he was wonderful, however—in a sense, he considered him a visionary—and included him on the program. Hiller's *Concert Étude* was rarely played, and in my judgment it overflowed with fakery. During the rehearsal, however, I listened to it from another perspective and changed my mind: it seemed clear and lyrical, less forced, much more coherent. Or perhaps the coherence was in me, in my soothed spirit. The conductor was German, and from the first chords one could detect an uneasiness, a secret disquiet, in Verret. At certain moments, instead of playing the piano, he seemed to be clamoring for an embrace, for a shock that would annihilate him and at last take away the pain, the stabbing pain that distorted his face and swelled the veins in his neck. At times he lifted his chest and raised his head as if waiting for the sword thrust that no one deigned to give him.

During that rehearsal Verret excited me more than he could have excited me with real caresses or words. I was certain that when he played he was thinking about us, about the night we had ahead of us, about everything he wanted and didn't want to ask me for. When the rehearsal was over and we walked outside, we were nervous and barely could hide it. We spent the whole time talking about music, like two maniacs; we linked one subject with another, we tried to rein in what we were feeling, and partially succeeded. When we reached the hotel we went directly to the bar. We both ordered whiskey, mine on the rocks and his with a splash of water. We were offered cigars and I decided to smoke one. I began to suspect that something was in the air between us, something unspoken that Verret was about to confess.

"My ex-wife called today," he said, not looking up. "She wants us to sell the house."

He was gathering his strength, gaining time, taking deep breaths to give himself courage. What Verret had to tell me, whatever it was, had nothing to do with his divorce, much less with the sale of a house. It's the kind of detail a woman can't grasp. But I could; I grasped it immediately and was prepared to wait patiently.

"I would have liked to keep that house," he added, taking a sip of whiskey.

We were very quiet; I didn't know what to do to give him courage. I couldn't ask him openly or beg him to tell me everything. And so I tried to encourage him with a gesture, with that and a few words: I brought my face close to his, leaning across the table, and confessed that I was happy I had traveled to Denver. He stared at me, and I saw apprehension in his expression, his eyes. I became frightened; I quickly swallowed some whiskey, and he did the same. Suddenly he looked away; he spoke as he looked at another table: "Someone's coming tonight."

I didn't understand right away. I thought about Australia and imagined someone was coming from there.

"I've arranged for a woman to come," he said, looking at me again, and then it could be said that I understood.

I understood only in part. It was a strange feeling, a mixture of annoyance and relief. Of hideous jealousy and deadly hope.

"What time is she coming?" I asked.

"She'll be here at eight."

I looked at my watch; it was six-thirty. I felt an impulse, or rather a temptation that was crucial to accepting subsequent events. Something in me longed to kiss Verret in the middle of the elegant Churchill Bar, in front of those gentlemen enjoying their cigars and discussing business. I told him so quietly, and he looked into my eyes.

"Do it, if you want to."

It was a moment of great tension, a pause so heavy with promise, attraction, and repentance that we didn't have to say a word. I didn't kiss him, but now everything had been said. I told him I was going to take a bath, and he made a feminine remark.

"Stay this way, with the smell of travel on you."

I wanted to respond in kind. "You too, with the smell of Hiller."

He looked up and sighed.

"Poor Hiller. . . . Did you know he fell in love with one of Mendelssohn's servant girls?"

I nodded, rummaging through the mists of memory.

"Mendelssohn's sister caught them—it was Fanny, wasn't it? A very tragic scene. Küchlin writes about it in his diaries."

"Küchlin?" Verret was shocked. "Do you mean Friedrich Küchlin? You must be the only person in the world who remembers him. I think he's a dreadful composer."

"But a great pornographer," I added. "He really was. I don't know of another creature who dared to recount copulation with his own grandmother."

Verret covered his mouth and spoke to me through his fingers.

"Maternal or . . . paternal?"

I winked at him and rubbed my knee against his knee: pure premonition beneath the table that concealed us.

At a quarter to eight we went up to his room. We were kissing when we heard the phone ring. Verret answered in a slightly hoarse, rather rough voice filled with desire, and we went on kissing after he hung up. A few minutes later there was a knock at the door, and we both adjusted our clothing and hurriedly smoothed our hair with our hands. An elegant woman, about thirty years old and dressed in business clothes, looked at us with self-assurance. She said her name was Lucy, and Verret, who had rehearsed his role very well, kissed the tips of her fingers and said his name was Robert. Then he introduced me: "This is my friend Ferdinand Hiller." The woman put down her handbag, looked around, and asked if she could use the bathroom. With a gesture Verret showed her the way, and as she passed by she gave him a kiss, a little kiss on the mouth.

And immediately used her little finger to wipe away the lipstick she had left on his lips.

One loses the notion of time under circumstances like those. I don't know how long she stayed in the bathroom. Verret and I continued caressing and began to take off our clothes. Who knows if she opened the door, saw us in each other's arms, and went back inside. Despite her youth, one could see that she was a prudent woman. There are moments when the magic should not be broken, not even to introduce another magic that's even better. Finally, there was a pause while Verret removed his trousers, and she reappeared, almost naked. It was the first time I had been involved in that kind of threesome. In my heart of hearts I was sorry the woman wasn't a musician. During the rehearsal with the Denver Symphony, I had noticed one of the cellists: she had a full, somewhat contemptuous mouth, but she opened it slightly when she played. It was one of those mouths that make you want to penetrate it, fill it by force while you spit out angry, unprovoked insults. If it hadn't been for Verret, who was enthusiastically playing Hiller's *Concert Étude*, I would have pursued that cellist.

The mouth of the woman we had in bed didn't open

with the same lewdness. For her to open it the way I wanted her to, she would have had to know music; would have to have mastered an instrument like the cello, for example, and become aroused as she performed an adagio, one in particular, from the Haydn Concerto, at the end of which—and I say this because I have proof—most female cellists are very wet, rabid and gentle at the same time. That infallible adagio is a miracle.

And I was thinking about miracles while one of them was happening beside me: Lucy withdrew her lips and showed me the giant she had rekindled in Verret. I couldn't control myself and I kissed her, I squeezed her breasts, I absorbed from her mouth all the flavor of the man who belonged to me. Verret began to moan and I left the woman to attend to him. I saw that he was extending a hand toward me, the right one, and moving his super-gifted fingers (somewhat tense, now) as if he wanted to reach me. I accepted his hand and raised it tenderly to my mouth: I licked it with pride, an admirable hand that was escaping from me, a humble hand that pulled marvels from the piano and now wanted only to pull marvels from an abyss: Verret's fingers went directly to my crotch and latched on, those fingers celebrated for playing preludes. My sex was unleashed—it grew until it hurt—but at the same time I felt something else germinating in me: thousands of capillaries swelled in my brain and filled my spirit; another erection of a very different kind was reaching completion inside. I kneeled on the bed. Verret, without pulling away his hand, leaned over and began to suck, so full of emotion and joy that I thought only about closing my eyes and dying without fear. As I was dying a warm caress kept me in the world: it was another tongue, belonging to the woman we had almost forgotten. It began working at the back of my waist and then moved down and buried itself between my buttocks, finding a way to push me even harder against Verret's mouth.

I decided to hold back; I shouted and snorted, I used my hands, my insignificant hands, worth so little, to caress and squeeze the back of the virtuoso. I didn't want to come, not yet, and so I separated from Verret and asked him to enter the woman: I just wanted to watch. He laughed, a provocative little laugh. I promised myself I would rip out his soul, I threatened to destroy him, without salves or saliva, drill him without mercy, just as he was. He listened to me in ecstasy and before he fell on top of the woman he tried to embrace me. I felt his hot torso, and our sexes brushed against each other; they hit at first without meaning to, and then we joined them intentionally in a silent, doubly intense round of fencing.

Verret sank into the other one. I stayed at a distance so I could watch his back, the movement of his hips. The woman called to me several times, but I refused to come closer. Her intention surely was to touch me, suck me while she kept fucking Verret. I ignored her but extended my hand and began to caress that snow-white back with its fine, hard muscles. I looked down: his buttocks resembled a woman's. I passed my fingers over them, first on the outside, and then I moved them inside a little. I didn't notice any difference. Verret moaned louder, he had felt me and begged me to keep on. I moved my fingers again, he stammered some words, he said "Yes" or simply "More." The woman thought it had to do with her and she said something, she moaned and said dirty words. Then I understood that I would do it, I knew it was then or never: I leaned over and kissed Verret's buttocks. I kissed them passionately, naturally; I squeezed them with both hands, as if they were breasts, and I opened them as if I were opening the universe. Verret trembled, a powerful electricity passed through his body, and under him the body of the woman shuddered too.

I was perceiving everything, understanding everything, licking with tenacity, as if that were the seat of my honor. When Verret's trembling calmed down, we calmed down too, the woman and I. The three of us lay quietly, embracing. I was still hard, inside and out, but I knew the pause was necessary, a moment for reordering and peace. Verret moved away and the woman asked me to take my turn. This time I didn't turn her down. I occupied his place almost instantly—the king is dead, long live the king—and I was glad to absorb some of his heat. The moisture on the skin of her belly was not hers alone: Verret's sweat was there too. And inside her sex, in the dark tunnel navigated by my sex, there were still pools of fluids from my virtuoso.

The woman wrapped her legs around my waist. I had the suspicion that she was trying to finish me off as soon as she could. But I, with a fixed idea in my head, was not about to give up so easily. Verret's hand caressing my back confirmed for me that he was waking up again. I kissed the woman and gently moved away from her. It was Verret I desired that evening, and the three of us knew it. He knew it better than anyone. He looked in my eyes and looked at my sex; he didn't say a word and he lay facedown. The woman did no more than whisper filthy things and caress us: she kissed my shoulders and kissed the face that was biting the sheets, the livid face of Verret, disfigured with pain and exhaustion. In his ear, above the woman's words, I imposed a fearful booming voice that I scarcely recognized as my own: I reminded him that I had kept my promise, that I was drilling him without mercy and would do it over and over again, as many times as I had to, with or without a whore, during the three days that our adventure in Denver would last.

I think he sobbed. It seemed to me that the woman was about to intercede on his behalf. I went mad at the final moment and bit his shoulders, the back of his neck that had always begged me to punish it. His reddish hair was in my mouth and I did nothing to remove it: his hair between my teeth had a strange effect on me, as if I had devoured an animal.

Afterward, Verret ordered drinks. The woman dressed and had a drink with us. We talked about the streets in Denver, what else could we talk about with her? When she left she gave Verret a little kiss and said: "*Hasta la vista*, Robert." But she said good-bye to me from the door: "See you, Mr. Stravinsky."

I STOPPED next to the wall, facing the bay, and looked over that section of the port that always brings back good memories. The day was a little cloudy, which made it a delight. I like the park—they call it Parque de las Palomas—it brings a very special kind of peace to me, which is why I try to go there alone. Once, many years ago, a woman went there with me. It was an act of madness, and in a sense, a magical act. The woman was Rebecca Cheng, the best clarinetist I have ever known, and I took her there to make music. Not with the clarinet, of course; that would have been too noisy. Rebecca played a Chinese instrument for me, a kind of tiny lute that produces a perverse vibration. She played it in a very sensual manner, moving her head as if she were in the Peking Opera. It was the middle of the week, close to midnight, and there was almost no one around except for two or three curious passersby who stopped to watch but, contrary to what I feared, soon grew bored and continued on their way.

Rebecca played Chinese songs, unfamiliar to me, but very beautiful. In the pauses between melodies, I kissed her forehead. I didn't feel capable of giving her any kiss more compromising. Not in that place, listening to the respiration of the pigeons, which was like the trees murmuring, and breathing in the smell of saltpeter, so strong that everything tasted of coarse salt to me: Rebecca's skin, and even my own lips.

When I was a boy my mother used to take me to that park. After my piano lesson we would visit one of my aunts who lived very close to it, on Calle del Cristo. My aunt would give me money to buy food for the pigeons. Late in the afternoon my mother and I would end up here. The pigeons would flock around me and peck at my neck, my hair, unexpectedly at my chest. There was an erotic image in that pecking, but I didn't know it. At the age of seven or eight, I also didn't know that in my life music, more than a pastime or a way to earn a living, would become an absolute dream, indispensable to sexual emotion. The few times I went to bed with a woman who didn't know how to play an instrument, I was infected by her ignorance: I didn't know how to touch her. I treated her with a certain disdain and ultimately left her unsatisfied. I thought there was no charm, no enchantment, and no need at all to root around that well of temperament which is the womb. I felt there was no profundity there, at least not the kind of profundity that interested me.

I looked at the horizon, cloudy but luminous. A common condition of the skies during these months. In the morning, early, I had been at the paper; I wanted to know Sebastián's opinion regarding the pages I had left him the day before. The story of Verret must have disturbed him, something I understand very well: Verret disturbed everything, even the peace and serenity of a man who never wanted—or was ever able—to stop being one. But I had also given Sebastián the story of Rebecca. I advised him to read it after Verret's. It simply had occurred to me that Rebecca was like those fruit sorbets that are served between strong-flavored courses to soothe the palate. There was an abyss between my passion for the Australian and the serene romance I had with the Chinese clarinetist. Just as there was an abyss between Rebecca and the whirlpool of mud, confusion, and horror that my relationship with Manuela became.

The result: Sebastián fell sick. Or he conveniently pretended to be sick to avoid facing me and therefore having to grant me the plenitude that my writing revealed. Before he saw me he would have to digest it slowly—like a boa constrictor swallowing down a large animal—and ponder the words he would use to comment on my two stories: first Verret's, which was more salacious, and then Rebecca's, which I imagined he wouldn't like at all. Sebastián detested girls—he detested children in general—and Rebecca, when she and I met, was not yet seventeen. Technically, she was a Chinese princess with a perfect ear, a musical genius capable of identifying any note out of context, and capable of producing it without errors or differences of pitch. That determination, that sonorous rigor, she then applied in bed to interminable couplings in which minimalism and delicacy made us increasingly voluptuous. I never knew if I went to bed with Rebecca or her ghost; everything was silhouettes, half-tones, sighs instantly transformed into shadows. Nothing was more pleasurable or more trivial, and over the years I often missed that love that seemed to float as if suspended by invisible strings.

In the park, surrounded by pigeons, I saw Rebecca again: I saw her there, and I saw her in bed, playing the tiny lute, naked, her legs crossed, like a slave girl who enslaves. Rebecca often said that she earned her living with the clarinet, but with the *sanxuan* (I believe that's the name of the instrument) she gained her place in heaven and won the submissive hearts of many men. Essentially, and this had nothing to do with music, she was a refined seducer who had already slept with half a dozen conductors—one of them very well known, a Japanese, apparently, who proposed a ménage à trois with a famous opera singer—not to mention her ardent interludes with all kinds of soloists, many of them Americans. Rebecca had lived in Chicago from the time she was a girl (that is, even more of a girl).

I have always heard that the old tend to rely on their memories. I always promised myself that I wouldn't fall into that trap. In the past I had brilliant days. Now that it was night—almost night—I refused to live like a vampire, drinking the blood of my own achievements. Recounting them in a book was one thing. Sitting in a park, surrounded by pigeons, looking at the bay and recalling a little Chinese girl who sucked exquisitely, as if she were painting a watercolor of pagodas, was depressing. It meant accepting defeat, or accepting death.

I stood up and smiled, thinking that the real corpse was poor Sebastián, dead of envy and remorse. How many marvels had he renounced in his life? How many times did he choose to close his eyes rather than open his heart and risk everything?

I, on the other hand, had kept my eyes wide open, like a guard dog. There was something in my nature that obliged me to savor, invite, propose with my eyes. And then, at a signal, an imaginary blow—ten cymbals from my master, Berlioz—I would attack without guilt or regret; the guilty are a race apart, inferior, of course. I would set only one condition: music had to be involved. A person has his whims; the fetishism of lips that have become muscular because they press against a mouthpiece, or the fetishism of thighs that, accustomed to surrounding a cello, are always full of fiery intuition.

I went back to the paper. I needed to continue; I understood that I needed to vomit up the passion that, however
equivocal and perverse, was still upsetting my stomach. I
was tense because I knew it was time to write about
Manuela Suggia: a flamboyant violinist, a demonic lover.

Manuela

WHEN SHE WAS a little girl, if she refused to practice the violin, her mother would force her to take off her shoes and stand barefoot on icy cold tiles. She did not permit her to say a word, not even to beg forgiveness. Manuela froze gradually, from her feet up to her head, and when she thought she could not endure any more, her mother would pronounce the magic words:

"César Cui, *Orientale*."

She always began with that piece. Manuela would put on her shoes and socks again, rub her hands, and run to get her violin. She would play *Orientale* in her own particular style, not taking her eyes off her mother, who leaned her elbows on the windowsill and looked out, her back turned to the girl, and as she listened she was tense, more than tense, she was indefinably furious.

"Dvořák, *Slavonic Dances*. Paganini, *Cantabile*."

She continued to request pieces in this way, with the coldness of a surgeon asking for a scalpel. Manuela obeyed and probably planned her revenge; all children plan revenge. Her family lived in Hamburg; her Portuguese father had been a sailor, and when he tired of going to sea he bought a small restaurant. Her German mother, also a violinist, but not a very good one, would mortify her methodically, an innate torturer. Manuela, of course, became a monster, a beast with exceptional talent, one of the greatest soloists I've ever heard.

At first glance you noticed nothing, though perhaps she was somewhat withdrawn. It was during intimacy that her learned cruelty blossomed, an aching sorrow that solidifies in childhood and never dissolves, not with love and not with revenge. She turned out to be dangerous, to herself and to those of us unfortunate enough to rest our heads beside her.

She was not particularly good-looking, with a nose that was too long and the mouth of a fierce duckling. Her eyes were very small—the kind of eyes that generally are associated with long, thin noses—and she had hair like cornhusks, terribly coarse and badly cared for. Her body was another story. She had cyclist's calves and a little bit of a belly—just a little bit; I've always thought that area ought to be soft. Her hips weren't German but very Portuguese, and she had sumptuous breasts with rosy nipples. If I hadn't liked Manuela for any other reason, not even for being the extraordinary violinist that she was, I would have liked her for her breasts, which looked like those of an adolescent—a robust German adolescent—and seemed to glisten. They probably had not been handled very often; I'm certain that men tended to reject her.

Rebecca Cheng once told me about the extremely high notes sung in Chinese opera that are inaudible to Western ears. In similar fashion, Manuela's malevolence might have been invisible to a spirit less well prepared than mine. She deceived many people, but not me. If I decided to have that romance, to eat out of her hand, to sink into her own particular swamp, it was because I found in her a musical element I never found in any other: Manuela Suggia played with hatred, with a merciless way of dominating the instrument, the music, and herself. All the vengeance she had promised her mother, and that she perhaps could not give vent to—the woman died when the violinist was fourteen years old—she poured into her performance. There was contempt, an inner demon clamoring for death. Manuela bled the melodies, that was the secret of her tragic sound: she pillaged them until they were drained dry.

Listening to her, I realized it wasn't true that art must always be practiced with love. Manuela was a consummate virtuosa, and her principal virtue was audacity, musical and otherwise; her great capacity for despising and, as much as possible, wounding. On the day I introduced myself in order to interview her, she smiled at me like an angel. I thought she was ugly, with her lank hair and pale cheeks. Then we both happened to be at a dinner party, our glances met a few times, she searched out my eyes, and I felt it was the moment to attack. We had already completed our interview, so I proposed talking with her for a while about her musical formation; it was a vile excuse, but it allowed me to accompany her to her hotel. Once there, we sat at the bar; she ordered an alexander, which is an old-fashioned cocktail, a drink for aging femme fatales. I ordered the usual: whiskey on the rocks. She spoke to me about her favorite composers and her teachers, and at some point the punishments her mother inflicted on her came to light. Winter in Hamburg is real winter: that little blond girl, barefoot in front of the open window, froze my own heart.

I listened to her in silence, sipping my drink and looking into her eyes. I saw a touch of perversity in the way she moved her hands, drank her alexander, and, above all, lied. It seemed to me she was lying, I suspected that she altered dates, names, unimportant events—unimportant, at least, to me—and that she did it for the simple pleasure of deceiving me. I had no way to prove it, but I'm a sly old fox. I've been one since I was twenty, and at that time I was forty, maybe a year or two older. My hair was still dark and my mustache intact; I didn't look too bad. Furthermore, I spoke Portuguese pretty well, and to impress her I proposed we use that language instead of the neutral English we had been speaking. An intimate atmosphere was established between us, and after the second drink Manuela's face no longer seemed homely to me. I suggested accompanying her to her room; she didn't answer. In a short while she got to her feet and tried to smile, but her irritation was apparent.

"Come on, then, if you want to."

I wanted to. She was staying on one of the top floors. As we rode up, alone in the elevator, I tried to kiss her. She pulled her mouth away, so I kissed her cheek; I placed my hand behind her head and drew her toward me. It was an awkward, cold skirmish, and I asked God to save me from being ridiculous. When we were in the room, Manuela disconcerted me. Without closing the door, she pushed me against the wall and threw herself against me; we were kissing passionately. Suddenly she stopped.

"Do your testicles hurt?"

It was as if she had kicked me right in the spot.

"They don't hurt," I answered. "Why would they hurt?"

"I always ask," she said. "Some time ago I met a man and one of his testicles hurt. Our date was ruined because of that."

She was laughing as she said this, and I had some misgivings: I wondered if it hadn't been a mistake to come up to the room of this lunatic. Manuela closed the door and began to undress; at the same time she tried to undress me too. I detected a natural clumsiness in her; her hands were trembling, but there undoubtedly was a good deal of pretense in her way of moving, of trying to seem modest. Her cyclist's calves were joined to powerful thighs, also a cyclist's, and higher up I caught a glimpse of her backside; I don't know how much of that she owed to a bicycle. Before I touched it I knew it was muscular and hard, a mannish ass that made me want to break it.

My role, at first, was entirely passive. I lay on my back and she embraced my thighs, buried her head, and began what was going to be an unpredictable sucking, at times frenetic and at times very sweet, almost childlike. I will not deny that I became terrified when I saw her lick my sex and enclose it completely in her mouth. I've read about madwomen who bite down at the moment of greatest rapture. That was why I feared Manuela, for I suspected right away that she was not very rational. I don't know if she was conscious of the fear she inspired in me. Perhaps she intuited it, like dogs who can smell who fears them and who does not.

"Let me know if I hurt you," she whispered, lifting her head hypocritically; the area around her mouth was covered with spittle.

"Move on top of me," I ordered; it seemed to me it was time for me to give some orders.

I grasped her by the arms and pulled. But Manuela was

not particularly docile—she continued sucking with frenzied eagerness; that woman had to do everything in a frenzy. Suddenly she sat up, then stood on the bed and looked down at me. She seemed to hesitate between dropping down or jumping on my chest and belly. I thought her capable of anything, even the most unexpectedly tender act, which is what she finally did: she squatted slowly, with exquisite lasciviousness, and sank onto my sex. Until that point everything was fine, but in a few minutes she leaned forward and bit my nipples; I should say that she chewed on them, a brutal provocation that drove me to push her back and throw myself at her. There would be no more coddling or affectation: I entered her in a frenzy and held her still by grabbing her hair. Then I had my revenge: I took her gleaming nipples into my mouth and decided to deprive them of their luster. I am not capable of chewing on a woman, not even a woman like Manuela. I sucked and bit her hard, I humiliated her by spitting at her, I spat on her breast and in her mouth. Then I turned her over— by this time she was very meek—and I bit the back of her neck; I entered her again, this time with so much animosity that I assumed she would bleed down there. As I penetrated her I felt a tearing, something I had not felt before, not even as a young man, the three or four times I had taken a girl's virginity.

The notion of having done harm, of opening a path through virgin flesh and causing pain, stirred me inside. I ejaculated almost without realizing it; I was still spitting at Manuela when my sex began to soften. I felt something sticky and warm on my belly; I didn't have to look to know it was her blood. I grew frightened and repented a thousand times over. It was the first serious repentance of the many that would overwhelm me during my lightning-flash affair with Manuela.

She was gasping for breath, and each time she expelled air, she also expelled a sigh. She made a move to turn over, but she did not even have the strength to separate from me. Then I decided to withdraw, and I saw the trickle of blood. I whispered that we would have to go to a doctor. She shook her head, she said there was only one thing that would comfort her. I assured her I would do whatever she asked.

"Come here," she murmured, pointing at her mouth; I imagined she wanted me to kiss her. "Put it here."

I realized she wasn't proposing a kiss. And I was about to tell her that I needed a few minutes rest (again I was afraid that she would bite me) when she raised her voice: "Piss on me, quick!"

I looked at the sheets, which were stained with blood and filth. I felt a ridiculous scruple: my urine would soak into the mattress; the chambermaids in the hotel would have to change it, they would engage in all kinds of conjectures. I hesitated for a few seconds, and this time Manuela was the one who spat: "Piss on me, imbecile."

I was confused, disarmed; for the first time in my life I felt fragile after coming inside a woman. I straddled her head. I held my sex in my hand and aimed at her forehead. I closed my eyes and leaned my head back. Not a drop. I concentrated. The seconds passed, perhaps the eternity of a minute. I strained to urinate; all I had to do was urinate. I opened my eyes and knew I couldn't.

"In my mouth," Manuela murmured. "Piss in my mouth."

I looked at my fallen sex. I was crossing a frontier and wasn't sure I wanted to. But she was pressing me, and I felt the cruelty of that pressure.

"Don't you know how to piss, you son of a bitch?"

I began to do it; I urinated in fear and rage. First a hesitant little stream and then a serious flood, all the urine in the world directed at her mouth, dirty bitch violinist. She was swallowing but some of the liquid spilled over, it went into her nose and ran out the corners of her mouth. I cannot recall a minute of my life that was filthier and more unfathomable.

When my urine came to an end, I got up in a daze and went into the bathroom, straight into the shower. I was still worried that Manuela would go on bleeding. There have been serious cases of homosexuals who bleed to death because of a bad fucking. I was afraid to become involved in that kind of scandal with a famous violinist whom no one would believe was so depraved. Which is why I was happy to see her alive, or almost. I was getting dried when she appeared in the bathroom; she staggered a little but her color was good. I asked how she felt and she shrugged. I asked if she had stopped bleeding, and her only response was to turn around and show me her backside. Her gesture seemed so vulgar that I regretted being there and having screwed her: having joined my skin to her contaminated skin. You could say that with Manuela I knew sensations, aversions, and repulsions that I had never felt before. Never until then had I regretted being intimate with a woman. I regretted it right then, while I was drying my back and Manuela, naked and sordid, strutted in front of me.

That night I got home by instinct, like a drunkard. My wife and daughter had already gone to bed. I sat down at the table in the kitchen, poured a glass of milk, and wanted to cry. I wondered if perhaps I wasn't the one who had really been hurt: if in fact it wasn't my flesh that had been torn by the power of a supernatural force. I promised myself I wouldn't see Manuela again, and I didn't even think about attending her concert. Before I lay down in bed I took another shower; I scrubbed my skin for a second time that night.

The next morning, as soon as I opened my eyes, I ran to the hotel. I called Manuela's room and asked her if she wanted to have breakfast with me. She answered, "You come up," and I shuddered. I went up and found her in a bathrobe. She had slept on the dirty sheets; a sweet scent of blood floated in the room. She ordered breakfast for two and we sat at the table on the balcony. I had a bitter taste in my mouth and the orange juice only made the taste worse. Manuela began to talk about other musicians and I realized that she told half-truths and, in general, a good number of lies. Before meeting her I had heard that as a condition for performing in certain venues, she demanded that contracts never be offered to the violinists on her black list. Without the slightest hint of shame she let me know that she presented similar demands to her record company, not only with regard to violinists but also cellists and accompanists who had earned her enmity. She tightened when she spoke of certain musicians; I had never seen such a capacity for rancor in any artist, least of all a soloist of her talent. That night, talking about a conductor with whom she'd had an argument, she confessed that she would have been capable of beating him to death.

"But jail," she added, "has always frightened me."

Manuela was like a dense stone of violence, a malevolent black hole that pulled me into her field, her dark, circular clouds. We went to bed after breakfast, and I can say that everything was normal and memorable. Then I went to my classes, and in the afternoon I saw her again at rehearsal. She behaved calmly and talked sweetly to the conductor; she had a thin little voice and spoke broken English with a ferocious German accent. When the rehearsal was over she said she wanted to walk for a while, and I took her to the old part of the city. She went into a jewelry store and wanted to try on a necklace; with a gesture she indicated that she wanted me to fasten it, and as I was doing so she remarked that she had decided to stay on the island for another week: she needed a rest and thought this was the perfect spot. My hands trembled; they were resting on her back as I tried to find the clasp.

"Does it bother you that I'm staying?"

I remained silent and felt her tug at the necklace; now she wouldn't allow me to fasten it. She turned around and looked into my eyes:

"I want to know if it bothers you."

I kissed her on the nose, her long thin nose that was always a little cold. I answered with a riddle: "I don't think it bothers me. It terrifies me, but only a little."

I paid for the necklace and put my arm around her waist when we walked out; we looked like a couple of wandering, complicit tourists.

After the concert she wanted to change hotels, which

pleased me. I suggested one on the beach, farther from the city and my ordinary environment: my house, the paper, the conservatory. I arranged to spend a couple of nights with her in that hotel. Manuela seemed relaxed; I would hear her thin voice and it would inspire certain things in me. Things I had never felt with any woman: repulsion, for example, and at the same time tenderness: in the middle of the night, a desire to cover her feet. We made love with fury, but also with gentleness and a great desire to live. Manuela took great pains to conquer me, though I didn't realize it at the time: I didn't know until it was too late. It was Sunday, and on Monday I had to return to my routine, especially to my house. We spent most of the day on the beach, and that night she suggested having supper in the room. After we had bathed she pulled me to the bed. We were both aware that for the rest of the week we would see each other for only short periods, and I wouldn't have another night when I could sleep with her.

She sat on the pillows, leaning against the head of the bed; she spread her legs and asked me to lay my head on her belly. I obeyed and she began to caress my neck, my chest, then my face. Closing my eyes and knowing that her fingers, capable of such infinite greatness, were touching me caused a joyful vanity in me, a state of euphoria, the hard drug that the combination of music and lasciviousness always is for me. Three nights earlier, Manuela had played Beethoven's violin concerto. She received a ten-minute standing ovation. I wrote afterward that not since the days of Fritz Kreisler had a Concerto in B been played with that genius, that overwhelming fire. A passage from the second movement came to mind, something that has always moved me deeply. She sat up, came forward, and reached my sex with her mouth, at the same time moving into a position so that I could kiss hers intensely. I settled my hands on her hips and forced her to press against my mouth: her sex moved around in my lips and I rooted in it until my tongue hurt. Manuela, as recompense, accelerated her caress: her lips moved up and down and I felt their devastating effect, the fury of a desire that rebounded inside my skull like a string rebounding against the neck of the violin, a torrent of savage pizzicati (in the style of Bartók): isn't that the dream of having music in your own flesh?

I went mad; I couldn't help it. I kneeled on the bed and turned her on her back so that I could enter her.

"Not yet," she shouted.

She jumped up, went to the closet, and came back with something transparent that looked like a condom. She dangled it in front of my eyes and I realized it was a glove.

"Put it on," she ordered in a voice that had changed; she changed it when she was planning some horror.

"Why should I put it on?"

I was burning with desire, but also with fear. I began to sense something distinctive, an atrocity that not even I could imagine.

"Let me put it on for you."

I let her. It was a very tight glove, lubricated on the outside. My gloved hand seemed slimmer and more retiring, almost feminine.

"Now, very slowly, put these four fingers tight together."

She was panting, speaking in a very hoarse voice, like one of the possessed who lose their natural voice and speak in the voice of some demon.

"Very slowly; you'll see, it's very easy."

She stood, leaned over a table, and offered me her buttocks. Panic began to choke me; I had sworn to myself I would never try anything like that. I stood behind her, passed my sex across her buttocks. But as soon as she felt me she whirled around like a wild animal.

"I want your arm!"

That was when she slapped me and I stepped back. I whispered that I couldn't, that she should let me do it in my own way, with my glossy prick bursting with desire.

"These four little fingers first," she repeated slowly, as if she were giving instructions on how to deactivate a bomb. "Then your thumb, like this . . . will you look at me?"

She pressed her fingers together and moved her hand through the air, along an invisible canal.

"Manuela . . ."

My voice sounded tearful. I wanted to fall to my knees, to plead with her not to subject me to this damned trial.

"Or would you rather have me do it to you?"

I could have left the room, of course I could have. Quickly put on my trousers and escaped with my shirt and shoes in my hand. But that wasn't in my plans. I was a real man, I always had been, I had never run from a woman, especially not this one. I wouldn't have forgiven myself then, and I wouldn't have forgiven myself today, when I've turned into a gossiping retiree writing this story that could end there, at that ridiculous moment, with my gloved hand hesitating before Manuela's sublime and very round ass.

"You won't regret it," she sobbed, or spoke as if she were sobbing. "It's a sensation . . . as if you were possessing my guts."

As if I were possessing her temperament, I thought, but possessing it seriously. Not as I had with the others, but profoundly, in her most intimate being, where blood and perplexity have their origin.

I closed my eyes. I had to decide in a second. I too had temperament. And mine was deep inside, still intact. Manuela roared: "Tear me apart now, damn it!"

"FIST FUCKING!" Sebastián exclaimed; he was pale and seemed tense. "Didn't you ever know any normal violinists?"

"Certainly," I said. "But they never wanted to go to bed with me."

He returned the pages on which I had recounted the first part of my story with Manuela. I suspected he had perspired while reading them; the edges of the pages looked slightly crumpled, as if they had been picked up by wet hands.

"And what happened after that?"

"I'm going to write it," I assured him. "But I need a break. This is too hard."

It wasn't even ten o'clock yet; we had both come in

very early, and the editorial offices were silent. Sebastián invited me to the cafeteria.

"You'll have some coffee, you'll wake up a little, and then you'll write the story of the violist."

I didn't catch it right away. My mind was elsewhere; it was enough just to mention Manuela's name, and something in me moved off, fled, flew far away.

"The one about the violated violist," Sebastián said more precisely. "The one who called his wife from bed."

The elevator doors opened and for an instant I recovered the image of that musician. Sure, sure, the violist. Very tall and neat, wearing polka-dot shorts and dark socks—I never could get him to take off those socks—and performing *Harold en Italie* for me, that woodland piece by Berlioz. When he finished, I caressed his back. He was skinny, and had charming skin and long arms that looked as if they were going to turn me around. Back then his only topic of conversation was the viola he wanted to buy, a Stainer that had belonged to Hindemith. He had a friend who was a friend of one of Hindemith's relatives. He had managed to put together almost all the money.

"Henri Kaestler," I whispered, savoring Sebastián's anticipation. "He was from Minnesota."

"Well, write about him," he said in that tone, a lustful tone of voice. "That way you can take a break from the diabolical bitch."

Sebastián sat down at one of the tables while I got coffee for both of us. Ibsen, the society editor, was in front of me, waiting to pay. She was carrying a tray with fruit and mineral water. I looked at her tits, fleshy and unrestrained, and thought there was no way to construct barcaroles like those on a diet of kiwis and baby bananas. She caught me in flagrante.

"Don Agustín, weren't you going to travel?"

If only she had played the piano a little, I thought. If only her mama, who gave her that doll's name, had thought to give her violin or flute lessons. . . . How I would have liked to go to bed with her; how happy I would have been to press the flesh of kiwis on her belly and between her legs and then feed on the green cream that flooded her clitoris.

"I'm finishing up some work I still had to do," I responded seriously, but my voice sounded somewhat cavernous.

"Your memoirs."

"More or less."

I went back to the table where Sebastián was sitting. I thought he would protest because the coffee was too light or too dark. He was an asshole who was never happy with anything.

"What did that idiot want?"

"Nothing important," I said. "She caught me looking at her tits."

Sebastián tasted his coffee; he seemed satisfied. I noticed that his tension had subsided a little.

"So then, are you going to write about the violist?"

"Kaestler." I raised my voice; I liked to make him suffer. "Austrian parents, a nice boy; he had talent."

Other retirees came in, people who were also clutching to this redoubt of normalcy. In the cafeteria it was possible to create the illusion that we were still expected upstairs.

"And his wife was probably a nice girl too," I added. "She had only one defect: she didn't suck or let herself be sucked. In Minnesota there are things that aren't approved of."

Sebastián chewed again with a dry mouth, that act of pure old age that irritated me so much. In my heart of hearts, perhaps, it made me afraid that at any moment I'd start chewing like that too.

"Did he tell you that?"

"Of course. Those kinds of confidences are never told to a woman. They're told to other men, to friends. Kaestler and I were beginning to be friends, but at the last minute he lost his nerve and turned into a little shit: he called Kathy—his pretty wife was named Kathy."

"You're a decent guy," Sebastián murmured. "In your place I would have rammed the telephone down his throat."

"Enough had already gone down his throat," I said without meaning to, and Sebastián gave a little start: a mystic smile lit up his face.

"Agustincito, why do you always have to be begged? Start writing, damn it. I can talk to Ibsen about giving you a kidney massage. Do you know she's studying massage? The feet in particular."

Ibsen, big-titted and innocent, was devouring her fruit at a nearby table. I looked at her with resignation: in many ways it was too late for me. But what he had said about feet reminded me of Clarissa Berdsley. That French horn player had the smallest feet I had ever seen on a virtuosa; they were in direct proportion to the astute little butterfly of her lower belly: a fragrant, diminutive, profound sex, like that of all women who dedicate themselves to the brass except, perhaps, the trumpeters—there are very few of them, but they're abusive.

"Not even massages . . ." I said suddenly, then immediately interrupted a sentence I would have surely regretted.

"Since you don't want to devote even a minute to the violist," Sebastián muttered, "please finish up the story of that filthy witch. I've never known anybody . . ."

He interrupted himself too. Remorse is a singular nuisance. Sebastián had never known a single person who did what he had seen only in magazines and on doctored videos. But I was there, a survivor of the extermination, drinking my coffee as if I had never offered an arm, my five gloved fingers, my desire to watch a woman disappear.

"A harpist," I remembered suddenly. "There was a famous harpist who disappeared in the snow. What a coincidence—she was from Minnesota too, like Kaestler."

Sebastián looked into my eyes; it was a look filled with compassion. I realized that he understood me.

"Her name was Lagerwall, Marjorie Lagerwall. She

called for help and nobody heard her. Since harpists speak so quietly . . ."

"Courage, brother."

"She froze to death. And I wrote an article about her. I said that as she was dying, surely she must have thought she heard a piece by Gail Barber, *Harp of the Western Wind*. If you're going to freeze to death, better do it to that music."

"Write it now," Sebastián suggested. "Finish telling me about Manuela."

"First the story of Clarissa Berdsley," I resisted. I had to resist in spite of everything.

"Whatever," responded Sebastián. "I'll help you even if you never tell me about it."

At that moment Ibsen, the unconfined queen of the fjords, walked past us. A little green drop hung at the corner of her mouth. It was the nectar of the kiwi, that putrescent liquid of lust.

Virginia

BUT OVER AND ABOVE Manuela, and Clarissa Berdsley, and any other adventure with man or woman, my passion for Virginia Tuten had not ended, and I could not leave her there, at the moment when she stands at the window again and performs the *Valse triste* by Nerval. That was the melody played by the musicians in his orchestra, in Prague, when they learned that Nerval, instead of going to the podium, had gone to a window and thrown himself into an eternal *valse* more dead than sad.

It was curious that Virginia would play it for me, looking suspiciously into the void. Most soloists, I really don't know why, have a morbid fascination with windows. Perhaps because they spend their lives practicing next to them, contemplating the landscape, yearning for the world that reverberates outside, while they play the same piece over and over again.

At first I thought I would stay in New York for two or three weeks. In the end, I was there only a week. Virginia visited me at my hotel and spent the afternoons with me whenever she didn't have a rehearsal. During that time, I also visited her in her apartment. She never invited me to stay there, but she gave me a key and I would go to see her early in the morning. I went in without making noise, walked to her bedroom, and woke her tenderly; then I would possess her without any special tenderness, but with rigor, exactitude: until the very end I thought I was doing it with cleverness. I employed my best weapons, all the ones I was familiar with. For the first time (and I'll bet for the last time in my life), I fantasized about leaving my wife and starting over again with another woman. That woman was Virginia, though the possibility of living with me probably never entered her mind.

When I arrived in New York, I found her reconciled with her secretary. The disagreeable Wendolyn controlled her day and night, organized her practice sessions and rehearsals, took care of her wardrobe, reprimanded her if she found her eating chocolates. She almost always behaved like a self-sacrificing wife determined to ignore passing affairs outside the home. To her, I was nothing more than a simple parvenu from outside the home. In the morning, when we were both in the apartment and she saw me sitting at the table with my shirt open, drinking coffee, her face would tighten. Even so, she never failed to smile and ask "How do you do, Mr. Cabán?" Then she would immediately take care of her business with Virginia.

One night I included Wendolyn in an invitation to supper. The three of us would go out, and I did this intentionally. I wanted her to have us close, accept us on an intimate plane, and recognize my superiority. The woman challenged me on a daily basis—Virginia could not avoid it—and I realized the time had come for me to confront her and for us to gauge each other the way animals in the jungle do: in front of the prey, the anguished flesh.

We went to a Chinese restaurant. Virginia loved noodles sautéed with nuts, and her enthusiasm when she heard the name of the restaurant—she didn't know where we were going until she heard me tell the cabdriver—was practically that of a child. She clapped her hands with pleasure, a slightly ridiculous gesture in a mulatta of her proportions, and her secretary gave her an ironic look.

In the backseat of the taxi, on the way to the restaurant, I put my arm around Virginia and pulled her toward me. My passion for her also drove me to puerile displays: I kissed her noisily, caressed her hips, and at a certain point I extended my hand over her shoulder, intending to touch her breasts. Wendolyn, sitting beside Virginia, began to look out the window. She was an old fox and knew that my actions were deliberate. From more or less controlled kisses I moved on to other exact sciences: I put my tongue in her mouth and rubbed her teeth with the tip, I reached her molars and wanted to continue on to her throat, I proposed asphyxiating her. Virginia, since she was so rustic, followed my game and lowed: her full mouth could not produce any better sound. I did more: I slipped a hand inside the neckline of her dress and with the other I caressed her thighs. I was attentive to the reaction of her secretary, who continued to look out the window. That indifference irritated me because it was both feigned and mocking, and I decided to crush her. With an effort, throwing myself almost on top of

Virginia, I put my hand under her skirt and forced her to open her legs. The noise my mouth made sucking at her mouth must have weakened the lustful she-lion, for she abandoned the view and dared to look at us. Virginia was moving gently, disguising the rhythm; she had one hand on my knee, but then I discovered that her other hand, looking for something to hold on to, had fallen on her secretary's skirt, and Wendolyn did not lose the opportunity to begin caressing her forearm.

I bit her on the neck out of revenge, I licked her cheeks out of love, and finally, when I sensed that she was about to be burned alive, I buried my fingers out of instinct. She raised her belly a little, tried to contain a circumspect spasm, and stifled a moan. Then she collapsed, her head falling back and then to the side. Toward Wendolyn's side, naturally.

A minute later the driver stopped in front of the restaurant. We got out with a feeling of exhaustion, and in my case of frustration as well. I felt a kind of depression; hope vanished during the meal, and I was certain that something, or someone, was excluding me from the picture. I was and was not in it. I saw Virginia devouring her steaming noodles, and out of the corner of my eye I observed her secretary, the only one who had decided to eat with chopsticks. It was she, and I see it clearly now, who was demonstrating her superiority to me. My love for Virginia—or if not love, my violent desire to rescue her—had blinded me completely.

Our supper was a wretched procession of attitudes: mine, defeat without my knowing it; Wendolyn's, obviously, voracious victory. And Virginia's—can I finally say it?—stupidity. Her life, at that moment, was reduced to her happiness over some noodles. Perhaps this is a condition inherent in virtuosity—I mean, a way of reacting with absolute imbecility to situations of great complexity or tension that have nothing at all to do with music. The truth is that in the cruel half-light of those little Chinese lanterns, Virginia was shrinking—and I was shrinking— her outline fading away like a phantom running down, or running out of God's grace.

When the meal was over we took another cab. There were no more erotic displays or noisy kisses between Virginia and me. Just frigid conversation, the whirlwind that can break you. I, in particular, felt demolished, exhausted. And exhaustion kept me from thinking, from evaluating the situation in its entirety: the trip to and from the Chinese restaurant, which had been like the trip to and from another country of unbearable brightness.

I left the two women at the door of Virginia's building. I kissed her and promised I would see her early the next day. The secretary and I said good night without kissing and without shaking hands. Her attitude was more defiant than ever, and when I left in the same taxi for my hotel, I felt a burning in my chest and face, and a stabbing pain deep in my skull. It was the loud banging of a story coming to an end. But I still didn't want to admit it.

I slept very badly. I dreamed about my mother, who had died when I was a teenager. I dreamed about my father, an amateur flautist whose real profession was designing railroad tracks. He was a road engineer, but he loved music as if it were the only possible train in a routinized, dreary life, and, after the death of my mother, a totally cheerless life, completely lacking in a woman's caresses.

It can't be said that I awoke. Rather, I came out of the stupor in which I had spent most of the night. I looked at the time: six in the morning. I calmly bathed and dressed. It was autumn, and the weather in New York was chilly. I went out wearing an overcoat, and walked for a long time.

The city was waking up too, and I wanted to think about what I would do with regard to Virginia. Then I saw a taxi and hailed it. I had the keys to her apartment in my pocket, and as I held them in my hand, I decided our situation had to be clarified that very day.

The night doorman greeted me; he was still waiting for his relief. I went up to the twelfth floor, opened the door with the same delicacy I used every morning, tiptoed across the living room, and went into the bedroom. Virginia was sleeping—what else did I expect?—covered by the sheets. It was Wendolyn, however, who lay there half-naked, uncovered, running the risk of catching a cold; her legs were spread and one of her arms lay across Virginia's waist. I stood contemplating the scene with a mixture of repugnance and childish desire. I felt like a little boy, or like an adolescent who lurks, sweaty and openmouthed, waiting for a miracle. I made a noise, and I believe Wendolyn opened her eyes, but I'm not sure. All I know is that I turned and left the door open behind me. I went to the kitchen and tried to prepare coffee. My hands were trembling; it was the first time they had trembled on account of a woman.

In that kind of situation a man can react in a thousand different ways. With anyone other than Virginia, I would have murmured an insult and left. In the best-case scenario, I would have gotten into bed too and slapped them both; I'm talking about slapping them lightly so I could then lick the place that hurts. But on this occasion I couldn't even manage to measure the coffee, pour in the water, or press the button on the coffeepot, the simple things I had done since I began having breakfast with Virginia.

I was about to leave it when I saw Wendolyn come in. She was in her underwear, and though I was dazed by my situation, I wasn't so dazed that I couldn't tell that she was thinner than Virginia, indescribably white, and nicely shaped. She also had enormous, quivering breasts, and I wondered—at that moment and for a long time afterward—what kind of duel took place between those two women when they held one another face-to-face, rolled back and forth breathlessly, and finally came, one torso crashing into the other.

"I didn't want to wake Virginia," said Wendolyn, in a tone of voice far removed from any arrogance or provocation; she knew she had won and did not even have to prove it to me. "She has a hard day ahead of her."

She was barefoot; she walked toward me, and I discovered that she smelled of Virginia.

"Excuse me," she said, taking charge of the coffeepot.

I stood there watching her, but above all smelling her sticky back. I did not need to touch it to know that her flesh had returned from a great battle. There was saliva and sweat all over her skin, and an abundant mixture of the fluids of both women, picked up by insistent fingers and then transported to other worlds: hair, cheeks, neck . . . Miserable necks that recognized each other.

I closed my eyes, came up behind Wendolyn, smelled Virginia again with an intensity now that left me no choice. I put my arms around her waist and felt her struggle, not with much conviction; the truth is she didn't even say no. She didn't say a word.

I turned her around so she stood facing me, and I kissed her breasts, I caressed them in a frenzy, and it seemed I was putting out a very old fire. At the same time I began to unfasten my trousers, and when I thought it appropriate, I put my hand on her head and pushed it toward my crotch.

She slipped down without protest, and I buried my fingers in her hair. She was a sorceress, an ambidextrous sow; she liked doing it with both men and women.

A short while later I shoved her to the floor. She lay face up, but I had other plans.

"Turn over," I panted.

She obeyed, of course. She also liked obeying her master's voice. She got down on her hands and knees, on all fours, her face humbled against the floor. I contemplated her for a few seconds and then I attacked; I did it so that she would feel all my wrath and all my fury. I was furious, and my sex was too. There's nothing that drills with greater pain, nothing that wounds so powerfully.

She screamed and that satisfied me. The second assault was terrible, and I'll bet she felt her uninitiated body breaking. Then I forgot about fury and anger, I even forgot about Virginia, and I surrendered to pleasure.

When I was finished, she collapsed. She seemed to be dying; she was moaning and babbling entreaties. I finished making the coffee, poured myself a cup, and dressed slowly. Without saying good-bye I slammed the door and desperately went down to the street.

It was still early and the sky was cloudy in New York. I didn't feel happy or sad, but I needed to walk. I recalled, I really don't know why, a song that my father used to play for me when I was a little boy. It was a record by a Spanish singer, and the melody was very classical, like a Schumann *lied*, though the composer was actually Rimsky-Korsakov. As I walked around Gramercy Park I seemed to hear it again, and I even hummed a phrase: "What is my poor heart worth to you?"

It took me several months to understand what that discovery was worth. And much more time, years perhaps, to annihilate the heart I had then.

Clarissa

PLAYING THE HORN is like performing fellatio.

I see the musicians, men or women, surround the instrument with their arms, place their fingers on the keys—the thumb of the left hand, for example, moves without modesty—and press their lips against the mouthpiece. Then I observe their expression, the half-closed eyes and tensed cheeks, and another image is superimposed involuntarily on the first: I see them touching the horn, yes, but I also see them licking, sucking, inflaming other singularly lukewarm pink keys.

This happened to me when I met Clarissa Berdsley. The first day I saw her, she was waiting near the dressing rooms to audition for the orchestra. She had blond hair pulled back in a braid, and wore a dress with little flowers on it. She was practicing, not looking at anyone, concentrating on the music, her body fairly erect. But those things, a straight back and concentration, never deceive me. There was a fire there—how could there not be?—a pair of small hands capable of retracing their steps and challenging taller, even thicker towers. I saw many possibilities as a woman in her—when I say woman, I mean someone who sucks implacably—and most important, I saw her cleavage and felt a kind of worm under my breastbone, a signal that always suggests to me that I am at the threshold of falling in love.

Intuiting the shape of her breasts, and at the same time seeing her so devoted to her instrument, seemed an erotic redundancy to me. She was practicing a passage from a piece by Strauss, and I waited for her to finish before introducing myself, announcing that I planned to write a note about the audition, and, incidentally, placing myself at her service.

She spoke extremely poor Spanish, but she let me know that the competition was strong, and the other horn players at the audition seemed very good. I placed my hand paternally on hers—I brushed against the horn, and the contact gave me gooseflesh—and told her I had a presentiment that she was the best.

It's incredible how ingenuous some virtuosas can be. Especially when they're from a small town called Menominee in Wisconsin. I know what those small towns are like: remote, charming hideaways where the girls, from the time they are very young, help their mothers put up fruit preserves. The spectacle can turn bitter, especially because in the process of boiling the jars, pouring in the blackberries, sealing the jars tight, and waiting for the snow, certain unexpected things can happen: the father, for example, leaves the mother; the mother, if she's young and still good-looking, suffers for the first few months but then finds consolation with a farmer, a widower. The girl, despite having helped with the preserves, will have to live at her grandmother's for a while—the mother will be busy with the arrival of a new baby, the child of the farmer—and the grandmother, so that the little girl won't be too much trouble, enrolls her in music school.

Clarissa began studying the oboe. After two years, under the influence of one of her teachers, who subsequently managed to seduce her, thereby breaking her precious maidenhead (beauties from Menominee tell all), she moved to the French horn. At the time I met her, she confessed that she practiced eight hours a day. She lived alone—a detail that made my heart palpitate, even though some of that palpitation ran directly to my lower belly—and had been in San Juan for two months, practicing the language and dreaming about the first horn player's chair, which would become vacant in September. There was nothing she wanted more than to live near the ocean, she said, and blushed.

Life has taught me that one never risks one's self-love, unless in the end there is compensation in the form of a woman who is aroused and good-natured. I thought about it for a moment and decided to attend the audition.

"I'm sure that next week I'll see you sitting in that chair," I murmured; I had leaned forward slightly to speak to her. "Whom shall I announce as the new principal French horn player?"

She not only was ingenuous, she was somewhat dim. She didn't react right away, and she looked at me in embarrassment. Suddenly she held out her hand.

"I'm Clarissa Berdsley."

Before I walked away to listen to the rest of the candidates, I finished her off with the sentence that had been simmering over a slow fire: "We'll celebrate afterward."

She smiled, and I realized she had even, very white teeth. I imagined her biting a stalk of celery or chewing a raw carrot; a healthy, virgin little mouth, free of germs but begging for fire. Now I had to ask God that she be chosen; I don't know if God was aware of my pressing needs or willing to become my accomplice in a symphonic-sexual deception. When Clarissa walked on stage for her audition, I reaffirmed all my plans. I found her sublime and wagered that her skin had a rustic fragrance, a mixture of milk fresh from the cow and the scent of meadows where raccoons fornicate: in short, the smell of the Wisconsin countryside. I thought that if I ever got her into bed, naked among the pillows, playing the horn for me, I would die of frenzy, of wanting to come a hundred times inside her blond and very hot sex, to lick the unlickable from the tip of her soul to the most unreachable purple place in her vagina. The deep purple, the essential conquest for a man. That and music, the real meaning of life.

Two weeks later, in a small restaurant near the theater, Clarissa and I were celebrating her appointment as principal French horn player. The conductor, impressed by her virtuosity (how could he not be?) suggested that she perform as soloist at a concert. She asked my opinion about the program, but the problem was limited to choosing between two works: the sonata by Dukas or the sonata by Hindemith. I listened without saying a word, and only when we ordered dessert did I dare to contradict her.

"It has to be Mozart," I said, falsifying my voice a little, using a tone I found intolerable but that undoubtedly was irresistible to her. "Everything begins with Mozart."

She put on the expression of a little girl who is caught dipping her finger into the jars of fruit. Finally she winked: "Then it'll be the Horn Concerto in B Major."

I answered:

"That's what it'll be."

A couple of hours later, we went to her apartment. We were in my car, and suddenly I heard her laugh.

"You're going to meet my roommate," she said mischievously, tossing her braid to one side.

"Let me guess . . . does it bark or meow?"

"Neither one," she whispered. "Once in a while he screeches."

"A parrot, then."

She didn't say anything else. We reached the apartment; she turned on the light and asked me to sit down. She explained that before she came to San Juan she had lived for several years in Florida. She had taught French horn there, traveling on weekends to work as a substitute in various orchestras. Her limited free time she had devoted to walking in the country, and sometimes to exploring caves.

I felt a stinging pain inside. Nothing important; I just distrust marginal pastimes. Music is an absolute that allows almost no distractions. Mixing it with fatigues and boots, and those helmets with lanterns attached that are used to light up stalactites, seemed shameful to me.

"In one of those caves I found a bat."

She stopped there, and there I felt myself become paralyzed. I looked at her; I had to look at her and hear the rest.

"It was a newborn and had fallen from the roof of the cave. It could have died but I saved it, and kept feeding it. Now it's like a puppy."

Now it's like a disaster, I thought, swallowing a tiny

mouthful of rancor. Ever since my early youth it had been clear to me that I would do anything to go to bed with a virtuosa. But in the general idea of "anything"—rows with deceived husbands, denunciations from histrionic mothers, tormented journeys by plane or by ship, treacherous stabs in the back, possible divorces—I never had thought of the possibility of caressing a mouse.

"Wouldn't you like to meet him?"

I spread my arms, shrugged my shoulders, tried to imagine the animal's head, its damp pelt, its wings flapping, the smell of the air it displaced.

"I'd love to see him."

She stood up and went to her bedroom, and in a minute she came back to the living room holding something dark in her hands. I noticed that it was much smaller than I had imagined. That calmed me.

"His name is Cumba," said Clarissa, looking at him with a mother's love.

"Doesn't he bite?" I asked, and at the same time I held out my hand; or rather, I held out my index finger and pointed at the monster's tiny head.

"I bite more than he does," she replied.

Her attitude had changed. Her shy disposition was transformed because of the bat. I blamed the bat because the same thing happened to me: suddenly my passion was so great, so engulfing and overwhelming, that I felt capable of anything, of kissing the animal and sucking Clarissa brutally; I had changed into the worst of vampires, in urgent need of her blood. A strange horn player brought to me by fate, a fierce combat granted to me by the devil.

I took off my jacket while she went to put Cumba away. She returned, undoing her braid, and I wondered if she realized the connotation of that gesture. She offered me a beer—she said she had nothing stronger to drink—and I accepted because the proximity of the animal had left a bad taste in my mouth. She drank water, only water, and at first we talked about music. I invited her to a concert on the following Saturday; a string quartet would be playing Beethoven. Clarissa was sitting across from me with her hair hanging loose—though you could still see the marks of the braid, waves like a siren's tresses—and her knees opened slightly, and she looked at me with what I took to be genuine fascination. I tried to catch a glimpse of some detail under her skirt—I wanted to know if she had on underwear—but I couldn't shift my eyes around too much. I dissimulated, talking about Beethoven's quartets, the opus numbers of his younger period, didn't she think that the influence people attributed to Haydn actually came from Mozart? Clarissa nodded, but I really don't know how much she heard.

"Pure Beethoven," I sighed finally, concluding some outlandish idea about a certain quartet being the best in the world. "Without stridency or sentimentality."

I said this and suddenly felt fatuous and despicable. I gave a start on the sofa and mumbled that it was time for me to go. They were magical words. I hadn't gotten to my feet yet but she had, and she came to sit next to me. She asked if I didn't want another beer. I sat there looking at her: was it or was it not time for the onslaught? I put my hand on her head, played a little with her blond hair. I said nothing; we said nothing. Tugging on her hair, I pulled her toward me and kissed her. I immediately searched for her smell on her neck and chest. It wasn't the odor of fresh milk mixed with new-mown grass in a Wisconsin autumn. In reality her smell was a perfume, I don't know which, a very nice one. But that stopped mattering to me when I unbuttoned her blouse and took out one of her breasts, the left one, if memory serves. I sucked it for a few moments and then took out the other one while I put my hand under her skirt. Just as I had imagined, she didn't have on underwear, and her juices had wet her thighs. It excited me to know that all the time we had been talking about the *Grosse Fugue,* she had been able to think only about a *grosse* poking. I went mad and tore at her skirt; I ripped it from top to bottom. There are two moments in the life of a woman that wound her mind like two burns: one is when a man tears something that she is wearing; the other is the moment of blinding fear when she is turned over, facedown. Over the years I have realized that those episodes hover near and sometimes return to haunt them, obliging them to find relief. I had no idea how long my relationship with Clarissa would last, but I wanted her to remember me for a long time, wanted her hands to perspire when she saw me coming to rehearsals, wanted her to feel like squeezing her thighs together and wetting her lips. And so, before I took her to bed, I slipped down and kneeled in front of the sofa. She raised her legs and hooked them over my shoulders. I smiled and leaned forward as if I were going to look at myself in the waters of a lake; I lowered my face, raised my tongue, which was my periscope, and traversed the shadowy bottom. Clarissa moaned, she pinched her breasts, and, above all, she called to me. The fool from Menominee wanted her punishment. I stood up and we went to the bed.

The room was in shadow. I lay down on my back and she was on top of me: eager for my sex, she tightened her lips against the heavy mouthpiece of my enchanted *corno*, which was about to leap with delight. In her way of sucking, of delicately moving her arms and making thorough use of her fingers (I could feel her fingers on my belly, and even from behind, trying to force the rear guard), there was a melody, a wealth of calls and fanfares, an uncommon art. Hungering in the dark wood, rising up in her saddle, Clarissa hoisted the instrument, the *corno da caccia* that summons us to pursuit, and from pursuit to gallant slaughter. Mad with passion, we slaughtered each other.

When everything was over she dropped beside me, breathing noisily, as if she had a bullet in her lung. I had been exhausted too; I knew I had come a couple of times, but no matter how hard I tried, I couldn't remember in what corner, in what little cave of her sweet flesh.

"Here's Cumba," I heard her say, and I opened my eyes.

The animal was flying very low. I remained still, waiting for him to go back to his cage, or all the way down to hell. Suddenly I saw him gliding, a repugnant little airplane that landed on one of Clarissa's thighs. She called him, she said, "Cumba, sweetie, come here!" And the animal crawled, it climbed up her body and approached her breast. Clarissa's nipples were round and hard, as small as beans. Cumba placed his mouth there and Clarissa smiled like a loving mother.

I closed my eyes again and thought we made a nice little family.

"Do you know what guano is?" asked Sebastián, giving me a smile that was ironic, but at the same time very tender.

"I knew what Clarissa was," I said. "A splendid wild animal in bed. That was enough."

"It's bat shit," he explained, paying no attention to me. "If it happens to drop in your mouth or eyes, you know, it's fever and lethargy for the rest of your life."

It was barely ten o'clock, but I had been at the paper since seven. I believe it was the first time in all those years that I had gone there so early. It was silent, and the ghosts of all the dead reporters were on the prowl. Nobody retired completely: retirees looked for any excuse to drop by the editorial offices. But the dead did not need excuses.

They wandered from desk to desk—Ibsen, the society editor, swore that she had seen them—and as they passed they pushed chairs and dragged ballpoint pens. At precisely eight-thirty one of the ghosts blew on some pages I had just collated. I was lost in thought, imagining that perhaps it was a good end for a sinister ending. Sebastián, however, refused to forget Clarissa.

"Who knows what she needed the bat for?" he mumbled. "Those midwestern women are very strange. . . . Menominee, what kind of town is that?"

She wasn't strange at all, just the opposite. After a time together, I could predict practically everything about her. I knew precisely what thoughts made her sad, the music she preferred, the food she would order. I even anticipated the words she would say to me from one moment to the next. The only place where she maintained her originality, her animal freshness, was in bed. But not for long. I satisfied my desire to see her sitting among the pillows, totally naked, playing the horn. And exactly as I had foreseen, I went mad looking at her, I kissed her a good deal and screwed her to the point of disaster. The disaster, sooner or later, is boredom.

"Do you believe in ghosts, Sebastián?"

He shrugged. He had the plush band in one hand and was turning over the bottle of bay rum on his desk. It meant that a migraine had begun to torment him.

"Clarissa did. She went to bed with me, but she loved a ghost: the ghost of a famous French horn player who had died years before."

"You've said it yourself," Sebastián remarked emphatically. "Horn players play as if they were doing it. The next time I go to a concert, I'll take a good look."

The ghost was named Dennis Brain. Clarissa showed me his photographs, obliged me to listen to his records, convinced me he was a genius, and I would swear he really was. She didn't even know him personally. The man died in London when Clarissa was a little girl.

"He was on his way to a rehearsal with the London Symphony," I said suddenly.

"Who? Who was going to a rehearsal?"

Sebastián's voice and his question gave me a feeling of déjà vu. He had used those same words before; we had been sitting in the same way and in the same place, facing his desk, surrounded by three modular walls covered with photographs.

"The ghost Clarissa was in love with," I replied. "Before he was a ghost, of course. He had finished playing at the BBC and was driving his car very fast, I don't know how many miles an hour. He was going like a madman, and not because he was late."

"It wasn't late for Manuela either," Sebastián murmured, and my eyelids twitched. It was a violent reaction I'd never had before. Fear, perhaps. And in a sense, from a great distance, sorrow.

"I was in the morgue and I looked up her obituary," Sebastián added. "Nobody dies like that."

"I didn't find out right away," I said in a very low voice. I felt as if I had been caught in a lie. "I was on vacation with my wife. I took along some books, and for days I hardly looked at a newspaper."

Sebastián noticed my discomfort; he tried to change the subject.

"Your wife . . . I'll bet you don't write a line about her. At heart you're a Puritan."

At heart, I thought, I was nothing more than a man trying to disappear slowly. That's what a song by Schoenberg says, I believe it's one of those cabaret songs: disappear slowly and die lightly. Manuela Suggia, for example, had died deeply, with all her being and all her spirit. And her madness had died with her. And in her consciousness, malevolence, and under the soles of her feet, fear. One dies with everything, with one's pajamas and one's passion. Schoenberg's song says that too. Or maybe the phrase is in a song by Loewe; I've enjoyed those songs very much. I had a friend who would sing them to me. She wasn't a virtuosa, but she conducted a small chorus in New York and learned certain ballads for the fun of it.

"If you don't want to write the ending," said Sebastián, "don't worry about it."

I was thinking about the voices in the chorus; about my friend, who was a coloratura, and about the passions beneath one's pajamas. My expression must have been imbecilic.

"The end of Manuela Suggia's story," Sebastián explained, raising his voice slightly. "You have no reason to ever write it. You still have a lot of stories to tell, happier ones for you, and for me. For example, that rococo violist . . ."

"I've already finished Manuela's story," I said slowly. "In fact, I was just about to give it to you."

I showed him the little pile of pages that a ghost had

disarranged. Sebastián opened his eyes wide, as if he were seeing delicious food.

"If you don't mind, I'll read them right now and let you know what I think."

"Not at all," I said. "It's early; I'll go to the cafeteria and be back in half an hour."

Finally he opened the bottle of bay rum and wet the plush band. He put it around his head.

"Shall I bring you some coffee?"

It was as if Sebastián were hypnotized; he looked up and answered with another question:

"Did you take up the story at the place where you stopped?"

I smiled and got ready to leave.

"Fist fucking . . ." I heard him murmur.

He added something else, but the words were altered when they reached me, as if they had come from the next world.

Manuela

"Now you rule," Manuela howled, her voice breaking.

I thought I'd never succeed, that if by some chance I did, repulsion and remorse would be so great that something would liquefy in my head. I was afraid I would collapse, that I would be paralyzed there, with half my forearm buried in her belly. To what depths of abuse, what chasms of savagery and madness was I descending?

And yet, when I heard her wail, when I experienced that soft sensation of having put my hand inside a fruit, something awoke inside me. It was not only desire, it was more than that: a mixture of desire and vertigo. Like a small, prolonged orgasm. Weak, yes, but incessant.

With a good deal of fear, I closed my fingers. Manuela had warned me that I had to be careful. If I scratched her, or tore her for any reason, she wouldn't be able to feel it (once inside, you don't feel anything), and then it really would be possible for her to bleed to death. When the tips of my fingers finally touched the palm of my hand, I squeezed hard, hard and happy. The closed fist was my great conquest. Manuela shouted without stopping, but I barely heard her. With my other hand I caressed my own sex, my perennial, accusatory witness, and then without warning I felt myself coming, if I can call it that. In reality, I felt myself going. The constant vertigo that had been plaguing me since I penetrated her was joined now by a total upheaval, like a surging tide, something I had never felt in my life before and have not felt again.

After I ejaculated I very cautiously withdrew my gloved hand. I suddenly suffered what I suppose was some kind of fit: everything looked dark, and I passed out; I urinated at the same time and lay in my own urine. Manuela, who was perfectly fine, leaned over me and blew in my face, and then she got up to find me something to drink—a soda, I suppose. The sweet taste turned my stomach; I knew I was going to vomit, and I asked her to help me get to the bathroom. It would have been absolutely degrading to vomit all over myself as I lay naked at the foot of the bed. In the bathroom, Manuela pushed me toward the shower. We both got in, I leaned on her, embracing her because I was afraid I would fall. Still, she seemed pale, and she confessed to me that she was in pain.

Two or three hours later, I said good-bye to Manuela and went home. I'm sure I was haggard, rigid, totally weak. I was like a little boy who has had a very serious illness: he doesn't understand the magnitude of the danger, he doesn't know that he was near death, but he senses that he has narrowly escaped something terrible and definitive. My wife looked at me in horror when she saw me come in: probably she had never seen me so ravaged. She followed me into the bedroom and stood looking at me as I undressed.

"What's wrong?"

I wanted to cry, first of all. Something, an idea perhaps, was boring into my brain, circulating through my veins, filtering in poisonous drops through all my organs. I had been invaded, infected in my cells.

"I think I'm dying."

My wife was used to almost everything: blond hairs on my fly, makeup stains on my shorts, clumsy stories, entirely unbelievable. But never, in all those years, had she heard me mention death. I saw her go on the alert; I transmitted some of my terror to her, because she came toward me and took my face between her hands.

"You're frozen."

I don't know if that was when the tears started. I suddenly found myself sitting on the edge of the bed, naked, sobbing as if I had just been told of the death of someone I loved. My wife rubbed my back, and when she thought I was calming down, she went to the kitchen to prepare a tisane. She brought me linden-blossom tea, something hot that helped to free my spirit. Because it was my spirit that had been trapped, held immobile inside an invisible fist. If at any moment during that brutal episode I thought I possessed power—over her innards, her temperament—now I realized it had all been an illusion. The belly that bore the traces of an invasive arm was my belly. And my mind, my sensibility, my common sense (if I still had any left) carried the mark of morbid fingers.

I slept badly, fitfully. I had nightmares, one of them about the death of Manuela Suggia. We were in a theater and somebody asked her to play *Hora staccato*, the macabre melody that pretends to be joyful but sells, or obliges us to sell, the souls of all of us who listen to it. I listened uneasily, I was suffocating in my dream. Until suddenly she said she would play "Petronius"; she said that name and looked at me. My anguish came to an abrupt end, and a melody began to leave her violin; at times it was tense and complex, but then it became transparent, graceful, so rich in overtones it made the air seem thick. I felt protected in an intact belly; the music of the violin was becoming warm, it had texture, a perfect sonority where ideas flew in and out like little birds. I was as happy as one must be when crossing the border into death. I thought I was dead. And just then I felt a blow: Manuela had disappeared. On the violin, which had been tossed to the floor, there was a black bow. When I saw this I shouted: it was a shout of horror that pierced my dream, the night, the simulated death, the presentiment of real death. My wife shook me and I awoke bathed in sweat, sadder and more fragile, my feet icy, needing to hear that melody again. The trouble is that the score of "Petronius" doesn't exist, or it has been lost, hidden away someplace, who knows where. My wife asked if I wanted a glass of water. I told her I'd get it myself, but instead of going to the kitchen I went to my study, stumbling and shivering. I took out ten or twelve notebooks, clumsily looked through their pages and tore one unintentionally, and finally found the notes on my trip to Boston. At the conference a German musicologist had referred to a dazzling violin solo that had been lost, and was called "Petronius," by Giovanni Battista Pergolesi, although confused references to it had been discovered much later in the papers of one of Paganini's followers. All anyone knew was that it was difficult and had a Latin epigraph; the musicologist recited it and I copied it down. I read the words aloud: *"Illa manu moriens telum trahit."*

I closed the notebook and went for a glass of water. When I returned to bed, my wife was still awake.

"This is serious, Agustín."

She said this in a tone of voice that let me understand what I had to understand: "This has gone too far," or "If you keep on with that woman you'll go crazy." I responded in the same code:

"I know. But it's passing."

The next morning, just as criminals or alcoholics relapse, I relapsed. I forgot about my horror of the night before and went to see Manuela. I had an excellent excuse: I wanted to know if she was alive. After the dream I'd had—that monstrous, miserable dream—I needed to be certain she was breathing, that her skin was warm and her voice capable of muttering any number of brutal words. When I called her room from the lobby, no one answered. Then I decided to go up, but I didn't even have the patience to wait for the elevator and I ran up the stairs. When I stood outside her room, I knocked twice. I heard her voice; she said something incomprehensible. Finally she opened the door: she was naked, and looked devastated. It was evident she had just awakened, and she looked at me with disinterest, as if she were still occupied by something left unfinished in her sleep. I asked her how she felt and she pursed her fierce duckling's mouth. She gave a half-turn and I couldn't help desiring her again, with a pain that was like weariness. I hurled myself at her and kissed her hair, the yellow straw that smelled of strange beings, of my sex and hers, and of a fistful of odors that undoubtedly had come from her aching belly. I grasped her breasts and bit her shoulders; she kept her back to me and I didn't see her face. I had no way of knowing if she was closing her eyes or looking off into space. I swore that I needed her and she whispered that she was dead tired and the only thing she wanted was to sleep.

"Fuck you," I said, turning her around and kissing her on the mouth; she was like a drug.

Manuela responded at first. But suddenly she moved away.

"There's a condition: you have to tie me up."

I grabbed her wrists.

"No damn conditions. Now I really give the orders."

There was the beginning of a struggle, but it must have been true that she was exhausted. She shouted obscenities; she shouted them in a Portuguese that sounded to me like Latin. At the same time she tried to bite me, kicking with her cyclist's legs, arching her waist, refusing to let me enter her. I spat at her, I insulted her with outrageous phrases, and when I finally overcame her and she felt me inside, she fell into a kind of languor. I went on insulting her for a few minutes, but then I began to calm down too, kissing her tenderly, telling her I loved her. I released her arms and she was still pliant and meek. That was worse, because then I realized that Manuela was really a vice, that her vacation would be over very soon and I wouldn't know how to live with this desire to murder her and eat her alive.

When it was over, we were two corpses. I didn't even have the energy to withdraw from her body. I licked her armpits like a dog, babbling the words that she had said first: "Out, out." After a while I summoned enough strength to get up and ask for something to eat. I had to go to the conservatory, but I was thinking only about when I would return. Manuela, in the meantime, took a long bath and got dressed. After she had eaten, she looked a little better. She said she would go shopping, and that we would see each other the next day. With that she did away with any possibility of our meeting at the end of the day. I was glad and not glad. On the one hand, I wanted to go home early, have supper with my wife, recover some normality, something that seemed so distant now. On the other hand, I was bothered by the certainty that Manuela was going to meet someone, or planned simply to go hunting.

I tried to maintain my equanimity. I was dying to ask if we could meet that night, but I knew it was useless. I could see it on her face, on her features that suddenly had become harder and more distant than ever. Everything was so violent that I decided to leave the room before she did. I didn't even ask her what time we'd see each other the next day. I was afraid of her answer, and I went out feeling diminished, a despicable and solitary creature.

I didn't see her again until two days later. She didn't look for me, even when she knew where to find me. And I decided, despite my desires—more than my desires, despite the obsession gnawing at my liver—that the best thing would be to let a few days go by. It was June, the weather was hot, and I showed up at noon. When she answered the door, she was ready to go to the beach.

"I have to make good use of the time that's left," she said. "You know I'm leaving tomorrow."

I said I didn't know and she burst into laughter.

"It's all the same," she added. "In any case, I wasn't planning to go to bed with you again."

I kissed her hair, her long, cold nose. She allowed it; it was her new tactic. I caressed her buttocks and began to lick her chest. I saw a mark on her neck and pulled back in order to see it more clearly.

"It was the night before last," she whispered. "A real man, with a first-class tool between his legs. Different from that little scrap of meat you have . . ."

She pointed at my sex, which at that very moment had begun to awaken. I pushed her, I stripped her—she was wearing only her bathing suit—I subdued her, but it wasn't the same. She knew it and mocked me. She did not show the slightest pleasure or compassion. Cold as a clam, she spread her legs and let me slip inside. I don't remember another encounter more insipid and graceless, not even with my own wife. Still, after coming like a dog— like a wounded dog—I wanted to encourage her and I talked into her ear. She turned her face, pushed me away, jumped out of bed, and put on her bathing suit again.

I wanted to vomit and I felt that I despised her. But at bottom it was a disdain filled with lust. I dressed, defeated, and offered her my hand. Her only answer was to slap me. It wasn't a slap of provocation but of real scorn, aversion, anger. The thing that left the hotel, under a sinister sun, was not a man but a ruin. I was lost—I've said it before—I thought I was incapable of ever feeling again, and months of absolute fidelity—I mean frustration— went by.

At last I overcame that phase in the arms of Alejandrina Sanromá, the angel of the celeste. From then on everything went better, outside and at home. After months of apathy I recovered the rhythm of my teaching, and I recovered, above all, the caustic tone of my writing. My wife, who at one point thought I was going to leave her, breathed more easily. My enforced fidelity, which she obviously was not accustomed to, had done her harm. She seemed withdrawn, abashed, shaken by the change in me. Then I decided to rectify everything, and when things had returned more or less to normal, I invited her to take a cruise. We went to the Virgin Islands (we left the girl with her grandparents), and my wife felt that our relationship had a new lease on life.

One morning, on the third or fourth day of our vacation, I opened a paper and saw the news. The violinist Manuela Suggia had committed suicide in El Paso, Texas, hours after playing Berwald's Concerto. I closed the paper, went to my room, and put it in my suitcase. I pretended I hadn't read anything, didn't know anything. Back home, a few days later, I opened the paper and drank in the rest of the story as if it were a cup of poison: after the concert, without changing her clothes, Manuela went to her hotel and swallowed some pills. Before they took effect, she lay down and placed a handkerchief soaked in chloroform over her face. That was how they found her the next day, with her face covered.

I was engrossed, the newspaper lying open on my lap. My wife found me; I couldn't stop her from seeing the article.

"Was she really good?" she asked, looking into my eyes.

"The best," I said, and bit my lip.

"SHE WASN'T a woman," said Sebastián, not looking up.

"Of course she was," I replied. "But we'd better leave it there . . . one shouldn't disinter the dead."

I suppose he felt a little uncomfortable. Perhaps the tone of my writing, the sick confession of those pages, had put him in a difficult position. While I was in the cafeteria, I dug up two or three more memories, all related to Manuela, and some small stories I haven't dared to tell yet. Then I went up to the editorial offices with a liberated feeling. I felt younger, less bitter. It occurred to me that when all was said and done I ought to travel with my wife, put an ocean between me and what had happened, and wait for my inner self to gradually reorganize.

"You have a life," added Sebastián. He said it in a tormented tone, as if he were telling me: "You have cancer."

"None of those stories is worth anything on its own," I protested sweetly, as if comforting a child. "There has to be a thread, Sebastián, something that goes from one skin to the other, without anyone's knowing it, of course. In the end, you're the only one who should see the stitch."

"And you've just seen it . . ."

He tried to be ironic, but I really was saying good-bye.

"I've been seeing it for a while. Ever since I began to write. And now you've seen it too. It isn't worth pretending: one dies twice. Or rather, our first death has to be organized in our own way, with our memories and our odds and ends, setting aside a single moment that's the key to everything. And when we have that, the other death can't touch us."

He gave an unhappy little laugh; he returned the ten pages I had left him and looked at me as if he were drowning.

"What will you do now?"

"Take a vacation. Aren't you taking one too?"

"At the end of the year," he said. He spoke with some difficulty, as if he were moved and didn't want to show it. "I want to go to Brazil. I've always wanted that."

A long silence fell; it was a kind of farewell. I thought of a piece by Fauré, the *Elegy for Cello and Piano*. If I had been obliged to put music to my life—to precisely that part of my life—there's no doubt it would have been the cello, which enters just a few seconds after the piano and erupts into an impossible melody, as ardent as it is visionary.

"And the violist?" a somewhat recovered Sebastián reminded me. "Do you think it's fair for you to go away like this and not finish telling the story?"

"Of course it's fair," I said. "But since it interests you so much, when I come back I'll tell you everything. I still have a few stories left in the inkwell."

Sebastián stood and gave me an affectionate look. I returned it. We had worked together for decades. Actually, we knew each other better than we suspected, perhaps better than we knew our own brothers, our own wives.

"Besides, Sebastián, think about this: what orchestra would be complete without a good conductor?"

I felt that he hadn't grasped the significance of my remark, but I didn't add another word. We went into the corridor together, and together we walked to the elevators.

"A conductor?" he exclaimed belatedly. "Don't tell me that you . . ."

"Austrian, of course," I answered with a wink, "I wouldn't have accepted anything else."

He put his arm around my shoulder. We were old and made a comic pair: Sebastián very skinny, and I a little overweight and round-shouldered. We zigzagged like a couple of tipsy compadres.

"I would have liked him to be Japanese," said Sebastián.

"None of that. Though I must confess there actually was a Japanese girl; do you know what a *saron* is?"

"A small marimba?"

"More or less. She was the flower of a single night. If you think about it, an incomplete night, because I didn't get to everything, and when I say everything—"

"That Austrian," Sebastián interrupted me. His voice grew fainter as the elevator doors closed. "I think that's where you should begin. Wasn't he the one who came to conduct . . . ?"

I'll bet the corridor remained silent. It was early, and only the phantoms danced along the walls: they were planning mischief, disturbing the shadows, pressing their ears to the cracks to see if they could catch one more detail. The end of a story, any story.

For the dead it's always the same one.